THE
MAGIC KEYS OF
TANGLEWOOD

THE MAGIC KEYS OF TANGLEWOOD

MALCOLM CHESTER
WITH
GABRIELLA LIPKIN

THE MAGIC KEYS OF TANGLEWOOD

Printed in the United States of America.

ISBN   978-1-949746-48-8   (Paperback)
ISBN   978-1-949746-49-5   (Digital)

Lettra Press books may be ordered through booksellers or by contacting:

Lettra Press LLC
18229 E 52nd Ave.
Denver City, CO 80249
1 303 586 1431 | info@lettrapress.com
www.lettrapress.com

Contents

Author's Note: This book began with some ideas from my wife's eleven-year old grandniece Gabriella Lipkin. We discussed the book throughout its writing. She gave me her opinions on what she liked and did not like and what to add and remove. She hopes one day to be a writer. She already has a good start. This book is dedicated to her, her sister Samantha, my grandchildren, Chase and Cora and all the other children in my life. Malcolm Chester.

Prologue

The young girl's breath came in short gasps. Fear gripped her, but she couldn't stop moving down the old tunnel toward a terrifying and unknown place. A voice in her head insisted she keep walking and the young girl seemed powerless to resist it like a zombie in some horror movie. In her bathrobe, the young girl had no idea how she arrived in this tunnel with its awful smell and electric feeling. The young girl should be in bed in her dorm room, not here in this nightmare, which she could not awake from. With the voice in her head becoming almost unbearable, the young girl reached a shimmering wall in a narrow corridor off the tunnel. She felt the power of the wall and knew she must finally stop. The energy from the wall burned her fair skin. Then, while she stood there, strange words reverberated in her head. The wall seemed to hear them as it suddenly disappeared in a bright flash. Once again under the control of the voice, she moved the few steps left to a large thick oak door. The voice in her head demanded she "OPEN THE DOOR." She began to do so, then suddenly stopped. The young girl worried this whole terrifying experience had something to do with the lock she grabbed on the gate. Her friends dared her to grab it and never one to turn down a dare she did so. With a better understanding of how this evil came to grip her, the young girl finally found the will to resist the voice. She took a step backward. With the voice now shrieking at her, the young girl took another step back. Sweat trickled down her face as she struggled with the voice in her head but she could feel the control of her limbs returning to her. Then the heavy door suddenly opened on its own to reveal a strange, weirdly colored, world inside. Truly frightened now, the young girl began to turn around when a hand that looked more like a claw with its blood red nails, reached from inside this smelly world and grabbed her gown. Before she could tear herself free, the hand pulled the young girl inside with tremendous force. The young girl screamed from deep inside as the big door shut in her face with a loud thud.

Skylar's Mansion

The three thirteen-year old girls, Peggy, Jade, and Carly, stared at the enormous house looming at the end of the long winding drive. They all lived in large houses in nice neighborhoods but this house looked like something out of a mystery novel. Pleasant smells from the large gardens filtered through the car windows. Their chauffer sat ramrod straight behind the wheel of the big black limousine transporting them, but showed some middle aged spread around his waist. Jade, so named because of her sea green eyes, pure white skin and jet-black silky hair decided the chauffer didn't merit one of her teasing remarks. Instead she turned to her friends and said what they all thought.

"Wow is this place for real? We have the biggest house on our block and it isn't as big as this house's garage. How many people live here?"

"Skylar told me once. We used to be inseparable in 6th grade but lately she is as close to the rest of you as she is to me. So we're the Fab Four now instead of the Dynamic Duo. Anyway, she told me that her mom and dad live here with her and her older brother but her brother isn't around much. He is away at college. Sometimes the other relatives come to stay but that is only on holidays. Her mom says they ought to sell the house and move into something a little smaller but her dad's family has lived in this house since the mid 1700's. He refuses to even talk about moving. Anyway, the most exciting thing about this place is its haunted, just like in a horror or mystery novel." Carly said, brushing back long strands of blonde silky hair from the front of her crystal blue eyes.

"Neat, I love haunted houses. Anyway, Skylar's family sound like royalty or something, but of course we don't have royalty in the U.S.— just rich people." Peggy said, rubbing her cocoa colored hands in front of her black sparkling eyes, long silky hair and perfectly shaped face.

"Yeah that's true but Skylar is related to some kind of duke back in England. So I guess she's both rich and royal." Carly added.

"Hah none of that impresses me, even the haunted house stuff. She is just Skylar to me. I'm not going to get hung up on royalty and money. They call my dad the king of the short sellers. So I guess he is royalty too." Jade said her chin pointed slightly upward.

"Well if you must know, my dad is head partner in a law firm. He is like a king to all the lawyers who work for him. He makes a lot of money." Peggy asserted as she moved a strand of black hair from her forehead.

"My dad has a big title too, Senior Vice President or something like that. He creates advertising for dog food, dolls, soft drinks, and pickles. A lot of people call him boss which is almost the same thing as king." Carly asserted as she stared out the window.

"Enough. Skylar is our friend. We just treat her like we always do. If she doesn't care about all this royalty stuff why should we?" Peggy said with some irritation in her voice.

Okay we won't, but I still feel like we're about to step into a haunted castle or something." Jade said.

The girls fell silent for a moment as the limousine pulled in front of the mansion's huge front door. The chauffer moved quickly out of the front seat and held the door open for the girls. Before the girls could even think about their luggage, the chauffer placed it next to them in front of the door. Carly grabbed the knocker, which she could barely lift and let it fall on the thick door. Moments later, a servant in elegant dress opened the door and waved the girls forward. As he did so the man said.

"I'll take your bags and put them next to the stairs. Then I'll find Skylar. When she tells me where you're going to sleep I'll take the bags there. I know she is anxious to see you. You can wait for her here in the hall."

After walking into the enormous front hall, the three girls focused on the heavy antique furniture, sparkling chandelier and large Chinese Vases around them. Then they looked at the dramatic huge staircase with large statutes at its base. Carly spoke while her normally talkative friends stood there with their mouths open.

"I've of course been here before. This place is like a palace or something. Skylar could care less. Even though we were best friends she didn't want me to come here. She felt too embarrassed. Really the best thing about this place is the large number of rooms. I think there are forty or something like that. You can explore forever. Oh and I actually thought I heard a ghost coughing last time I was here, but Skylar says she never heard a coughing ghost."

"Hearing a ghost would be neat but this place is far too stuffy for me. There is only one way to break the tension of staring at this place and all its expensive things. Watch this." Moving her bag aside, Peggy suddenly started doing cartwheels and flips. Her last flip landed right next to a big Chines vase. The vase began to rock back and forth, when Peggy's right leg hit it. Carly, close to where Peggy landed, leaped for the vase just managing to stop it from falling onto the polished marble floor.

"Wow just in time. This vase is from some Chinese dynasty. Mang or Ming, something like that. I think it's worth a lot of money. Anyway no harm no foul. Although I must say those were very good cartwheels and flips. You're great at the gymnastic thing you do." Carly said wiping her brow in relief.

"I think we ought to calm down a little. We don't want to wreck Skylar's house before she even gets here." Jade pacing nervously and staring at an embarrassed Peggy said.

At just this moment, a tall and regal looking Skylar appeared at the top of the stairs. She had on a long cocktail dress and some pearls. She started to slink down the stairs, her large dreamy vivid azure blue eyes focused on her friends below. Her long luxuriant red hair picked up the light from the second floor lights, as did her creamy white skin. As she descended, Skylar spoke with a fake high society accent.

"Darlings, so good of you to come by. I think we have some tea in the drawing room if you'll follow me."

Jade, who loved to play dress up ran to the top of the stairs followed by Peggy and Carly. Jade began to sway her hips as she followed the still slinking Skylar downward. The other two girls did the same thing. Carly started laughing.

"If I sway my hips any harder, I think I'll dislocate them. Does this really attract boys like it's supposed to?"

"Yeah it does. You know Thad the hunk. In the sixth grade, every time I passed him in the halls at my Junior High, I start swaying my hips. Even though he pretended not to look, I could see him watching me." Jade said with a twinkle in her eye.

"I wasn't at your school but I saw him at the park in his swimming trunks. No boy should look that good at age fifteen. It isn't fair. If I date him, I'd have to watch other girls all the time so they didn't hit on him." Peggy said.

"Good luck with that! If you date a guy like Thad you'll have to accept that he is going to be a two or more timer." Jade laughed then continued. "What do you think Skylar?"

"Boys, boys just like toys to play with darling. A little wiggle here a little wiggle there, you can have them all." Skylar said her head high in the air.

"Okay enough play acting. The Fab Four are all here Skylar and ready to have a great time. The question is are you ready for us?" Peggy said with a big smile on her face.

"Am I? I've been waiting all day. I put on this outfit to welcome you in style. We're going to have a good time in this big old house, I can guarantee it." Skylar said losing the accent and smiling from ear to ear.

"So what do we do? It's only 3 pm, plenty of time for some activities." Carly said.

"I have an idea! When I was little I used to slide down the bannister, but it's really tricky. Before you reach the statutes at the end of the bannister, you have to jump off. Otherwise you hit the statutes and believe me that hurts! I'll show you if you want. Anyway we can't be sophisticated all the time. Sometimes we just have to be kids." Skylar said as she ran back up the stairs. Skylar continued. "Now watch this."

Skylar jumped on the bannister, put her arms in the air and slid quickly down toward the end quickly gathering speed. At the last moment she pulled up her dress and rolled off the bannister onto her feet, staggering to control her forward momentum. When she finally stopped moving, Skylar yelled.

"A perfect 10—well maybe a 9 but whatever the score that was great fun."

Peggy at the top of the stairs slid next almost as well as Skylar, but her rolling dismount put her on the floor. She quickly leaped to her feet to show everyone she remained uninjured and commented "I guess that was only a 7 or so but it sure felt great."

Jade followed soon afterwards moving down the bannister much more slowly but when she rolled off the bannister she managed to stay on her feet before hitting the wall. Jade her head held high and said, "That had to be an 8 at least."

"No way, you went much too slowly." Peggy challenged.

As the two girls glared at each other, Carly moved down the bannister very slowly, her eyes focused on the statute at the end. Like the rest, Carly tumbled off the bannister just before the end but fell on her side with a loud *thunk*. Carly sustained no major injuries but the pain still registered on her face. Carly trying to maintain her dignity managed to say. "So okay that slide wasn't the best but I never slid down a bannister before. At least I made it in one piece."

"That you did my friend. Okay we've shown we can still be kids. What's next? We have a pool, a gymnasium, a large grass area, and a horse stable. We can do whatever you like." Skylar announced in a strong voice.

"The pool is good for me. I want to try on my new bikini." Jade said.

"Good for me too, but I only have a two piece. My mom won't let me wear a bikini." Peggy added.

"Try a one piece. My mother still thinks I'm a kid." Carly complained.

"Well if you must know, I have a two piece but it's pretty skimpy. I guess Jade is the only one here who can show off." Skylar said with some reluctance.

"Really, what difference does it make? We're only wearing the suits for each other. Now if Thad were around, that would be a different story wouldn't it." Jade said.

"Whatever, let's go to the pool. Grab your suits out of your bags. You can dress there." Skylar said as she waved them forward down a hallway to their left.

A half hour later the Fab Four gathered at the side of the pool carefully examining how each of them looked in their bathing suits. Jade made the first comment.

"Eat your hearts out boys. We all look terrific. Even you Carly in that one piece look great but I see hints of a bruise from where you landed after sliding down the bannister."

"No problem there. It doesn't hurt much and makes me kind of glad I have on a one piece. I don't want you staring at the whole bruise." Carly commented.

"It'll heal in no time. I want to get wet. The last one in is a rotten egg." Skylar said as she jumped into the pool.

Jade and Peggy jumped in next splashing in the water and laughing. Carly lined up on the side of the pool and dove cleanly in the water. She emerged seconds later into a powerful freestyle stroke. In less than a minute, Carly reached the opposite side of the pool and did a perfect flip turn. She came to the surface and leaped out of the water into a strong butterfly stroke. Carly quickly reached her friends. Her friends stared a few minutes; then Peggy spoke.

"What was that? Are you trying out for the Olympics or something?"

"Yeah are you trying to show off?" Jade added.

"Nothing like that. My parents have a cabin on a lake in New Hampshire. From the time I could walk, I spent most of my time in the lake swimming. I joined a swimming team at school and competed in a few meets. I did very well, won most of them but got tired of spending every free moment I had swimming. I'd much rather be hanging with you than drying my skin in a chlorine pool."

"Yeah, we all have things we've done. Peggy is a good gymnast, Jade danced in some ballets and I rode horses in meets. There are reasons we are the fab four." Skylar said with a slight smile on her face.

"Yeah you're right. We have to be able to do things if we are going to be girl superheroes. So now that we're in the water what's next?" Peggy said.

"I know. We'll line up on the side of the pool. I'll call out a boys' name. Then each of us will walk like they do in the beauty pageants. The sexier our walk the more we think the guy is hot. Since we've already talked about Thad we will start out with him. I'll go first." Jade said as she climbed out of the pool.

"I think all of us will do our sexiest walk when it comes to Thad but okay Jade show us what you have. I have never played this game before but it sounds like fun." Skylar laughed.

The girls loved the game. Each boy they knew received different treatment, some like Thad caused pronounced slow exaggerated hip movement while others like Stevie, the class nerd and brain in Jade's school, received no hip movement, tiny steps and arms crossed in front. As with Jade, the girl mentioning a boy had to do the first bathing suit walk for him. As the girls lived in the same general area but went to two different junior high schools not all the girls knew a given boy. In such a case they just copied the girl who knew the boy. After twenty boys received reviews, Skylar put up her arm and said.

"Okay we've walked for almost every boy we know. My stomach is getting sore. Let's decide who is the sexiest boy. I vote for Thad."

"So do I," Jade quickly agreed.

"And me," Peggy added.

"Not me. I'm not big on muscle guys. I vote for Peter. He is good looking and sensitive." Carly disagreed.

"Okay Thad wins 3-1 but I agree a little with what Carly said. Peter is very good looking. He'd be my second choice." Skylar said.

"And mine." Peggy added.

"I don't know Peter but if you guys say so Peter can be second on my list too." Jade said nodding her head. After the show, the girls jumped in the pool and splashed and laughed the rest of the afternoon.

Later that night after playing more games and having a delicious dinner, the girls gathered in Skylar's enormous room. They all carried flashlights and took turns making their faces look like devils. They talked very quickly and giggled so much Peggy got the hiccups. Although the girls should have gone to bed an hour ago, none of the girls looked or acted tired. After another hour, Skylar's expression suddenly changed as she leaned into her close friends.

"Since you're all going to Tanglewood with me next year, I have to tell you the legend of the witch."

"Wow a real live witch—that sounds like fun. Please tell us. There is nothing I like better than a spooky story." Jade said.

"Okay but it will take a while."

Looking around, Peggy laughed and said.

"We don't have anywhere to go, so let's hear the story."

"First I have to tell you a little about my family. My father's relatives fled England in the early 1700's. My great, great, great, god knows how many greats, grandfather was the Duke of Lancaster. Somehow he got on the wrong side of King George and had to get out of the country. With his inherited fortune, he began a shipping business in Boston, which over the years branched out into many different manufacturing and transportation businesses. He became one of the wealthiest men in the American Colonies. In 1735, he began building this house and another one for his sister Prudence. It took twenty years to build both of them but they started living in the houses before they were finished. The Duke had several children including a daughter, Samantha.

"As they didn't have many schools then, the Duke's sister Prudence with the Duke's support began teaching the duke's daughter and other girl relatives in the second large nearby home during the day. Because of the old twisted oaks on the property, Prudence named her home Tanglewood. Other wealthy families in the Boston area, many of them friends of the duke, began to send their daughters to Prudence for what they believed to be finishing school type instruction, which included table and parlor manners, posture and conversation training. Prudence, while providing this instruction to young girls, also included some literature, math and science instruction in her teaching. She along with the duke possessed large and highly respected libraries and Prudence strongly believed in sharing her library with the young girls that came to her house. In those days, girls didn't go on to college but they had to be smart and polished in the social graces to attract wealthy and educated men. Many wealthy boys, who were expected to attend college, attended private schools like Briar Manor, which more closely resembled the private schools of today.

"At our age in 1750, Samantha began attending her Aunt Prudence's classes at Tanglewood. In 1752 when girls outside the family started to take classes at Prudence's home, Samantha began to fight with a girl named Elizabeth, the daughter of a wealthy banker in Boston. The fights grew worse. Samantha, the most popular girl in the class played a number of mean tricks with the support of her friends on Elizabeth. After playing a particular mean trick on Elizabeth, they spilled ink all over the front of her dress before the boy she liked called on her at Prudence's school, Elizabeth told Samantha and the other girls in the school she had great powers as a witch and would curse them and the school. Samantha and the rest of the girls laughed at her threats and made life even more miserable for her.

"Elizabeth, unable to take it anymore, left Prudence's school. No one heard anything about her until the next Halloween when she suddenly showed up at the school in the middle of the day. Before the adults sent her away, Elizabeth told anyone that would listen that every year on Halloween one of the girls in their class would disappear. They would be sent to a place between this world and heaven, the so called World in Between, where they would stay until someone found the key to the lock that would appear on the front gate and let them out. The keys would be hidden on the school property but it would take magic to find them. Elizabeth also warned everyone that if they destroyed or tampered with a lock or put a key other than one of the magic ones in it, this person would be sent to this strange world and be forever imprisoned there.

"After Elizabeth left, Samantha disappeared that very night and a lock appeared on the gate. The duke attempted to have Elizabeth arrested and tried as a witch, but her parents escaped with Elizabeth to Australia where they built a new life among the settlers there. Each year thereafter on Halloween, another girl would disappear and another lock would appear on the gate. The girls at the school swore they saw Elizabeth dressed in a white gown every Halloween even though she lived half a world away in Australia.

With witchcraft involved and girls disappearing, the little school soon ran into difficulties. Classes shrank as the wealthy refused to send their daughters to Prudence. To save the school and find his lost daughter, the duke sent a team of soldiers to capture Elizabeth and bring her back to Massachusetts, but he acted too slowly. With the vicious gossip about the cursed school reaching all corners of the state, Prudence had to close the school. She even stopped giving instruction to her relatives. Unfortunately, girls who attended the school continued to disappear every Halloween night. Finally, the soldiers captured Elizabeth and brought her back to Prudence's home in 1774. The soldiers left Elizabeth's two children and husband in Australia. An angry and defiant Elizabeth when confronted by the duke refused to lift the curse on Prudence's little school and its students. Even the duke's promise to send her back to Australia at his expense did not change Elizabeth's mind.

Desperate, the elderly duke hired a witch from Salem, Rachel and brought her to Prudence's home, where the duke held Elizabeth. As soon as Rachel arrived at Tanglewood, she threatened to use magic against Elizabeth if she did not agree to lift the curse. Elizabeth laughed at Rachel and attacked her with a powerful spell. Rachel fought back. The duke and Prudence fled Prudence's home as the two witches hurled spells and fire at each other. When the duke returned two hours later, both witches had disappeared. The duke ran to the front fence and sure enough two new locks hung on the gate.

After Elizabeth and Rachel disappeared the part of the curse that took girls every Halloween ended. No more girls disappeared at Halloween. The school reopened as before and took the name Prudence gave her home. In 1830, Prudence's daughter, who bore no children, willed her property to a board of directors to house a girls' school forever after. Under the new board, Tanglewood continued to grow and prosper and eventually became the most prestigious private girls school in the country. To this day, the key locks hang on the Tanglewood School Fence next to the entrance to the school."

"That's a terrific story but it can't be true can it? I mean girls disappearing and locks appearing, that 's the stuff of fairy tales." Jade commented.

"Well, my father, who told me the witch story many times, swears it's true and the old locks still hang on the fence. I've seen them. So you tell me." Skylar answered.

"That's just so creepy, but after all this time someone must have tried to do something with the locks." Carly asked.

"They did. There are twenty-six locks on the gate instead of twenty-five. In 1771, a Briar Manor boy cut one of the locks to rescue his girlfriend. It didn't work. He disappeared and a new lock appeared on the gate. After that the school put an iron cage around the locks so no one could tamper with them. Very few have in all these years. Oh and by the way, the locks aren't even rusted after more than two hundred and forty years. No one can explain why that is. Even more troubling, just last year, a girl named Tiffany disappeared and a new lock appeared on the gate. So the curse is still very much alive. Tiffany had a reputation for doing crazy things. Some kids claimed she climbed the fence and tried to open one of the locks. The school called such a notion silly. They explained the new lock as some kid playing a stunt, maybe even Tiffany herself. Still, Tiffany remains a missing person. No one knows where she is. "

"The Fab Four has to do something about these locks. Maybe we can free the trapped girls, especially this Tiffany. With most of them being over two hundred fifty years old maybe they wouldn't be able to live in this time but at least they could go to heaven. It's a noble quest." Jade said.

"Yeah it may be a noble quest but remember, one of the locks traps Elizabeth in the World in Between. I wouldn't want to let her out. Since I have the same last name as Samantha she'd do something terrible to me I know it." Skylar said.

"Don't worry, we'll avoid letting her out. I'm sure there is a way to tell which lock is hers." Peggy added.

"Yeah maybe." Skylar said as she crawled into her bed. "Anyway, I have a whole bunch of things planned for us tomorrow. It's late. Let's get some sleep."

"Okay but if it gets too creepy in my room I'm coming back here." Jade said.

"Yeah me too. A place like this has to have ghosts." Peggy agreed.

"I've never seen or heard one, but my dad says that a very nice beautiful fourteen year old girl supposedly haunts the place. She has long dark hair, a perfect oval face and beautiful crystal blue eyes. She died of whooping cough. So if you hear someone coughing that's probably her, but my dad thinks she crossed over into heaven many years ago and no longer haunts the place." Skylar said with a naughty smile on her face.

"I have a feeling if I hear coughing it will be one of you trying to play a joke on me." Carly complained.

"We wouldn't do that," the rest of the girls said, laughing loudly. After the laughing died down, the girls slowly made their way out of Skylar's room and down the long hall to their rooms.

Next Day

At breakfast served in the huge dinning room by another well-dressed servant, Carly looked at Skylar and the rest of her friends with a smile forming at the corners of her mouth as she ate a piece of fragrant bacon. Carly said.

"Okay who coughed last night? Three times you woke me up. I even heard your footsteps the last time. Skylar it had to be you. It's not funny."

"Nope, it wasn't me. I fell asleep minutes after the three of you left. I didn't wake up until 7. Once I fall asleep a brass band in my room couldn't wake me."

"That makes two of us. Sometimes I wake up at night but last night I slept like a rock. I didn't wake up until 7:30." Jade added.

"The same thing happened to me. I read for about twenty minutes then fell fast asleep. I didn't wake until 8. I guess you heard the ghost. Maybe she hasn't crossed over to heaven after all." Peggy added.

"No way. It must have been one of the servants." Carly said.

"I don't think so. The cooks and chauffer don't sleep here. The butler does but he stays on the fourth floor and doesn't come downstairs at night. All the windows and doors are fitted with alarms. The guard patrols at night but he almost never comes in the house. Anyway, I saw all these people yesterday. None of them had a cough." Skylar said.

"I refuse to believe I heard a ghost last night. This isn't a story or a fairytale. This is real life." Carly complained.

"I'm just telling you what I know. You can draw your own conclusions. Anyway, we have to get ready for our first activity, horseback riding. You'll need to have on jeans and a comfortable shirt. I have some extra boots if any of you need them. I do hope you can ride." Skylar said with another one of her teasing smiles.

"I ride but the last time I did I got a very sore butt." Carly complained.

"I ride too but only at summer camp. Those horses are so tired and lazy it isn't much of a ride." Jade laughed.

"Hah Skylar, you don't have me on this one. I've been riding for two years. I even jump. I'm actually pretty good at it." Peggy said proudly.

"Then you and I will gallop through the pastures after we all take a trail ride around the property. Of course the rest of you can come with us if you want but from what you said maybe you won't want to." Skylar responded.

"No I'll stop at a trail ride." Carly said.

"Yeah me too." Jade agreed.

An hour later, the girls walked their horses through Skylar's many acres of horse trails. Skylar looked very comfortable on her horse, Peggy a little less so; Carly and Jade appeared uncomfortable. Jade complained.

"Honestly, when you have a comfortable car with air conditioning and leather seats why do you need to ride around on sweaty horses with biting flies?"

"Because it takes no skill to sit in a car while it does require skill to ride a horse. It's a sport." Peggy answered.

"If some handsome boys rode around on horses I could see it but not many boys ride horses around here. Now out West that's different. Some of those cowboys look pretty good." Jade responded.

"Jade I think you have boys on the brain. Most guys are jerks. They want one thing. At least that is what my sister Sue says." Carly added.

"Then why does Sue spend all her time trying to attract Ralph the captain of the high school football team. I saw her at the town pool. Let's face it ladies. We're teenage girls. We look at and fantasize about teenage boys and young men; that's what we do. Teenage boys do the same thing. They sit around and fantasize about us. What do you think Skylar?" Jade asked.

"I don't like to admit it but it's Cory for me. He already goes to Briar Manor, the boys' school that started about the same time as Tanglewood.

He'll be a sophomore next year. Briar Manor boys usually date Tanglewood girls. It's been that way for hundreds of years." Skylar said.

"What does Cory look like?" Peggy asked.

"A little like Thad but he's a soccer star and the football team quarterback. When he practices soccer, I watch him from a hidden spot close to his field. He always looks great." Skylar answered.

"I hope he has some good looking friends." Jade said hopefully.

"I'm sure he does. Anyway you'll find out at the first mixer. The Manor boys will come to Tanglewood at Halloween. The Halloween dance has been a tradition at both schools for hundreds of years." Skylar answered.

"Cool. Hey I'm getting a little bored riding this way. Skylar are you ready to do some real riding?" Peggy said.

"Of course, I know the way so I'll take the lead. Are you other girls alright with the two of us going for a gallop." Skylar asked.

"We are. We'll head back to the stables and wait for you ladies there." Carly said as she looked at Jade to get confirmation.

Seconds later, Skylar took off at a full gallop. Peggy followed her but held on tightly. Skylar looked at home on her horse, Peggy didn't quite look the same way. Within minutes, the two girls disappeared into the forest. Jade spoke.

"I hope Peggy doesn't get hurt. Skylar can ride circles around her. Peggy shouldn't have bragged about her riding like she did."

"Yeah. I worry about that too, but there is nothing we can do about it except wait and call for help if they take too long." Carly said.

An hour later, Peggy and Skylar rode their horses into the barn. The horses looked tired and sweated heavily. Skylar appeared as her usual chipper self. Peggy appeared tired and nervous. When she dismounted her horse, she could barely walk. Her legs shook. Skylar called out.

"Let me give the horses a little food and water then we'll snack a little. A horse boy comes at one. He'll rub the horses down and make sure they're okay. Did you ladies feed your horses and give them some water."

"Yeah thanks to Carly. She knew the routine from the last few times she came here. I'm starved." Jade said.

Later that day after an afternoon running around the field playing soccer and hockey and an excellent meal of roast chicken, the girls settled in for the evening. They watched a movie with their heartthrob, Seth Williams, who occupied a space on all their walls, and like the last night spent over an hour talking and gossiping in Skylar's room.

During a lull in the conversation, Skylar jumped up.

"Hey girls, I have a Necromancer set a relative bought me for my 12th birthday. I've never used it before. Maybe we can summon the house ghost?"

"Cool idea, sounds like fun, but what in the heck is a Necromancer." Jade said.

"Someone who can raise the dead I think." Peggy said.

"Yeah that's right. Now let's open this box. It has all the ingredients we need." Skylar said. After they removed all the materials from the box, Skylar continued.

"Here are the directions. Light four candles at nightfall and cast them to the four directions. Hey that's great we are just in time, the sun set a few minutes ago."

The kit had a compass and the girls used it to put one candle at the west, one at the east, one at the south and one at the north. The girls used some matches near the fireplace to lite each of the candles. They also put the kit's pentagram inscribed on a large plastic cloth on the floor. The pentagram had all sorts of cool inscriptions on it. Each of the five points had a label. One said Spirit, the next Earth, the next Fire, the next Water and the final one Air. When the girls finished, Skylar continued reading.

"Place a glass of water at the base of each candle. Then place human bone, hair or fingernails in a copper bowl and ignite. Place the bowl in the center of the four candles thereby completing the pentagram of negative space."

"Okay I'll offer up some of my hair. I have a wild end here and have been meaning to cut a little to even it out." Carly said.

Carly used a pair of scissors on Skylar's dressing table and cut a piece of her hair. Then she placed it in the copper bowl provided in the kit, which the girls put in the center of the pentagram. Carly used a match to light it. The girls then filled the small glasses that came with the set with water they kept in plastic bottles and placed them next to the candle. Satisfied Skylar started reading again, holding her nose a little. Burned hair smelled bad.

"Lay a solid line of moist Earth in a complete circle, then lay another circle of common salt."

"Jade and Peggy quickly completed these tasks with materials in the kit. Skylar stood up and addressed the girls.

"Okay now I am going to read the incantation. When I am finished we all have to say very loud and fast, "Wa Ta Na Siam five times. Then each of us has to extinguish the candles. Are your ready?"

In unison all the girls said "Yes" almost screaming with delight.

"Okay here we go. "Hic en Spiritum; Sed Non Incorpore, Evokare Lemures de Mortius; Decretum Espugnare; De Angelus Balberith; En Inferno Inremeablis." Then raising her hand she along with the other girls Skylar said five times,

"Wa Ta Na Siam."

After uttering the phrase five times all four girls chose a candle and extinguished it.

The four girls waited several seconds then they heard from the center of the pentagram a distinct cough. Excited, Skylar spoke to the center of the pentagram.

"My distant relative please talk to us now or make another sign of your presence."

"Yeah talk to us," Jade added.

The girls sat for almost ten minutes but nothing more happened.

Finally Peggy said.

"I think that's it for the night but we all heard the cough didn't we? I mean that was really something."

"Yeah even though I was hoping for more, I think we actually heard from the ghost. Remember she had Whopping Cough." Skylar added.

"Yeah that was really neat but I'm beginning to feel a little tired." Carly said.

"I am too but it's a bummer. We all have to leave tomorrow," Peggy complained.

"Yeah I could hang here for a whole week, playing during the day and evoking the spirits at night. " Jade added.

"I'd love to have you here but all of us have to report to Tanglewood for orientation on Wednesday three days from now. We need the time to get organized and pack. My dad and mom are finally coming home just about the time you're leaving. I want you to meet them. Anyway, we'll have to do this again sometime. The school is only two kilometers from here. You can see the school from the top of my house. So, we can come here if we get a little break from school. Heck we could walk." Skylar said.

"It's great having you as our friend Skylar. I'm kind of nervous going off to a boarding school. Having your house nearby helps me feel a little more secure." Carly said.

"Yeah me too. I went to camp earlier this summer but that was different. It was only for four weeks and we didn't have all the academic pressure." Peggy added.

"I don't know about you girls but I can barely keep my eyes open. I want to get up early so we can do some things before we have to leave." Jade said.

The girls all nodded their heads and slowly walked toward their rooms as they did the night before.

Ghost

Several hours later, Carly woke when she heard a loud cough very similar to the one she heard earlier at the Necromancer ceremony. Moments before, she dreamed of a handsome boy riding a horse toward her. Carly had on her prettiest dress. In the dream she frantically thought of what she might say when the boy road up to her. Sitting up in bed, she looked around the room but no one sat or stood there. Still, Carly sensed someone or thing occupied the room with her. Her long blond hair nearly stood on end when a strong clear voice spoke to her.

"Can you hear me? I sense you can but I'm never really quite sure until the person I'm trying to haunt answers me."

"I can but if you're a ghost I'd rather not hear you. It's scary. Are you the ghost that's supposed to haunt this place and coughed during our ceremony earlier this evening?" Carly answered.

"Yes I coughed at your ceremony. The ceremony gave me just enough power for all of you to hear me. Ordinarily only people with a psychic gift can hear me. My name is Constance. I've haunted this place since 1850, which is one hundred sixty four years ago. I died at age fourteen of the Whopping Cough. It's been forty years since I had anyone with whom I could converse. Skylar's my direct descendant but she doesn't have the psychic gift like you do. Neither do any of your other friends. I have been so lonely that I thought about entering the light and crossing over to the other side." Constance responded.

"You speak kind of formally, like one of our English lessons. I guess that is the way people talked in your day. Also, I don't understand what you mean about entering the light."

"Yes I listen very carefully to people speak so I can understand modern language but still I find myself speaking more formally than most people. As to the other thing you referenced, I need to explain a little about ghosts. When I died, I found myself as a spirit outside my body. I could move about the house and hear what everyone said but as is true now I could only speak with someone who had the ability to listen. I could move through objects as well as the air but for the most part I couldn't move or affect them. From the moment I entered the spirit world, a bright light burned above me. I somehow knew that I could enter the light and pass into another world, but if I did I couldn't return. So I never wanted to go in there. I felt much more comfortable here. As time passed, I found that if I tried very hard I could affect objects. For example, I could move something light like curtains a little. If I did so, however, I became very weak. The weaker I became the stronger the pull of the light. The first time I experimented with moving things, the light almost pulled me inside. A week went by before I gained my normal spirit energy again.

"As time passed, I watched other people die and enter the spirit world. Most looked around a little and then flew directly into the light. They didn't want to stay. A few stayed but even though I tried to tell them about conserving their energy, these ghosts would eventually try too hard to move something or to communicate with someone who couldn't hear them and then disappear into the light. Some also liked to do ghostly appearances, but those appearances also require a lot of energy. I saw one ghost do an appearance, look at me with a sense of accomplishment and then fly seconds later into the light. Oh and there is also another kind of spirit: an evil one. I saw only one. It was very angry, tearing around the house, but it used up its energy very quickly. When the spirit did, it flew into a swirling red and black light that looked like a whirlpool. I can tell you that light looked terrible and evil. I assume this spirit went to Hades, the dark place."

"Wow if everything you say is true that is really neat, but since I'm in bed maybe this is really a dream."

"No I assure you, you're wide awake. If I remember correctly you just dreamed of a handsome boy on a horse, a really nice dream. I can't dream anymore but I can sometimes see dreams of sensitive people like you." Constance said.

"So you were snooping on my dream. I don't know if I like that or not. Maybe next time, I'll have a nightmare. You won't want to snoop on one of those dreams."

"No I won't. When I lived, I frightened very easily. I'm still that way. I haven't changed in all these years."

"Okay so what do we do now? Do you take me off to some magical places or what." Carly asked.

"No but I can show you the house like no one else can, all forty five rooms of it."

"I thought the house only had forty rooms." Carly said.

"They only use forty rooms now, but there are five more that they don't use. When my great grandfather the duke built this place, the place had only thirty rooms but each of his descendants either added rooms or refurbished the rooms that were already there. That is what is so neat about this place. We have many different styles in various rooms and extra rooms should they ever be needed." Constance said with some excitement.

"Wow could you show me the unused rooms? That would be neat."

"I'd love to do that. Now follow my voice in your head. We'll turn left when we leave your room. Oh and I will put on my glasses. When I read in real life, I wore them, but not when boys or men could see me. Most of the time I don't put them on because it takes energy to wear the glasses, but if I do you can follow the glasses floating in the air. Even though you're a sensitive, you can't always see me." Constance said.

Carly could barely keep track of where they went. At first she travelled through normal rooms some of which she had already seen, but then they entered a very grand room with tall ceilings. Constance instructed her to push on a panel on the far wall. To her great surprise, Carly entered a series of closed off rooms. Large sheets covered the furniture dust appeared everywhere so much in one room Carly could see her footprints in it. More than a few spiders had spun webs in the corners. The rooms had a very stale smell. Still, many of the rooms appeared to be quite grand. Carly couldn't understand how anyone would let the rooms go to waste. Carly's favorite room, an ornately decorated library with carved wooden shelves, held some fascinating books. Carly could have spent hours combing through the dusty old volumes. Constance said her dad used to spend hours in the library and for that reason she also liked the library more than any of the other unused rooms.

Several hours passed in the great adventure but eventually Carly became tired. She addressed Constance.

"Constance I'm too tired to explore anymore. I need to go to sleep. Tomorrow afternoon, I have to leave and the rest of the girls want me to participate in the morning activities we've planned."

"Oh no, I'll never see you again. I'll be alone. Can't you stay a little longer?"

"No but I have an idea. Why don't you follow Skylar to school next week? Then we can be together at the school. I assume you know all about Tanglewood."

"Yes of course I do. I attended the school for a year before I became sick.

Still, I'll be scared in that big old place. Somewhere in the tunnels underneath the school lies the entrance into the witches' world where the keys are kept. If I get stuck in that world, I'll have to go into the light. "

"You know about the Tanglewood Keys."

"As a part of this family, I most certainly do. I even explored the tunnels under Tanglewood looking for the witches' world and the keys while I attended the school just as almost every other girl there did. I almost scared myself to death walking around those tunnels but I never found the keys or the witches' world." Constance said.

"Things are different now. You're a ghost. You scare other people. You shouldn't be scared of anything." Carly observed.

"No, I've never scared anyone in my whole spirit life. And of course I become scared. As I already said, there are dark things in the spirit world. I haven't found out very much about them in all these years and I don't intend to do so now." Constance said.

"Okay Constance but will you please come to the school with Skylar next week? You're already my friend and I don't want to lose you." Carly pleaded.

"All I can say Carly is that I'll think about it. I've been in this house a very long time. Maybe I need a change of scenery." Constance said slowly.

"Okay that is good enough. Now I must really get back to bed. Will you come along with me?" Carly asked.

"No I think I'll rest here awhile and take off my glasses. I've done more tonight than I have in some time. I don't want my energy level to run down."

"Okay goodbye then. I really liked being with you. I think we'll see each other again very soon."

"I'd like that," Constance said as her voice faded away.

After Constance left, Carly quickly returned to bed. She fell asleep as soon as her head hit the pillow.

Last Day

On the morning, Carly woke late. The other girls had already eaten breakfast. Although very tired, Carly felt excited. She wanted to share her experiences with Constance the night before.

When Carly finally ate breakfast and caught up with her friends chasing each other on a large grass field, she could barely contain herself. Before she could say anything, however, Skylar spoke as the rest of her friends gathered around Carly. They were covered with sweat and smelled a little.

"You certainly slept late. We came into your room and tried to wake you but couldn't. Did you have trouble getting to sleep? That happens to me sometimes."

"No I spent half the night exploring your house with Constance, the ghost you talked about when we first came here. When we all heard the cough that was Constance. The ceremony gave her the power to talk to all of us for a moment or cough so we could hear her but it quickly faded. Ordinarily she can only talk to sensitives like me." Carly answered.

"Impossible! The story about ghosts haunting this place is just that a story. Sure we heard a cough but I figured one of us did it in a way the others couldn't tell. Also, my Necromancer game is only a game. How could it make the ghost stronger? Still, it puzzles me that you know the ghost's name. According to the story, Constance is the name of the ghost." Skylar said.

"She told me her name. She claims she died of the Whopping Cough in 1850 at age fourteen. She also showed me where the mansion's missing rooms are located." Carly replied.

"Once again what you say is completely accurate. You could have found out about Constance on the internet or from a book but only people in the immediate family know about the hidden rooms. Granddad and Dad both wanted to open them, but the architect told Granddad he would have to tear down most of the wall in his favorite room. Then the architect said all the rooms would have to be scrubbed, and the wiring and pipes replaced. Granddad and dad both decided they didn't want to spend the money. I don't suppose you can show us how you slipped into the rooms." Skylar asked.

"Sure I can. It's easy, follow me." Carly said.

The Fab Four walked hurriedly into the house. Just as they did so, they bumped into Skylar's parents Edward and Britney, who had just come in the front door. The three girl guests quickly introduced themselves and thanked Edward and Britney for allowing them to stay for a few days. At the end of the pleasantries, Edward had a question.

"You girls seemed to be in a terrible hurry when we bumped into you. Where were you headed?"

"Dad you're not going to believe this but Carly spent most of last night with Constance. She showed Carly a way into the forgotten rooms. Carly wanted to show us this hidden entrance." Skylar responded.

"You girls look serious. Of course, I know about Constance but if she exists as a ghost, which I seriously doubt, why would she reveal herself to a person outside the family?"

"Mr. Worthington it has to do with her energy level. If she tries to communicate with non-sensitives, she has to use too much energy. She risks being taken into the light, which is the passage to the other world where people go when they die. None of you are sensitives. I am. She can talk to me without using much energy. I know it's hard to believe. At first, I didn't believe in Constance either. So why don't you follow me to the hidden entrance. If I show it to you, you'll be more likely to believe me. After all, how else would I know where the hidden entrance is located?"

"Lead on Carly. I'm fascinated with this whole thing." Edward said.

"Edward I don't know if I am. This stuff about a ghost is ridiculous, but I suppose there isn't any harm in us following our guest to this supposed hidden entrance." Britney said.

The four girls and Skylar's parents formed a line behind Carly as she talked.

"Okay here I go. I left a piece of red ribbon I had on my wrist at the exact location of the hidden door. I thought I might be leading some people to it today. Now let me concentrate so I can remember how we went."

Carly remembered the route well. Within five minutes she came upon the ribbon poking out from behind a lamp in a very ornate room. The room had twenty feet painted ceilings. Pictures, carvings, elegant hand painted wall paper and polished wood panels adorned the walls. Carly hadn't realized the rooms' beauty the night before. Carly put the ribbon back in her pocket and felt along the wooden panel behind the lamp as she did last night with the help of Constance. To her great surprise Constance whispered in her mind.

"The wall is so well fashioned you have to reach your hand up higher to find the one place where you can feel the edge."

With a big smile, Carly did as instructed and immediately found the edge. With a little push the door swung inward. Carly stepped inside and waved everyone else forward. Mouths open, the girls and Skylar's parents walked inside and started to explore. Carly held back a little so she could speak with Constance.

"Constance thanks for helping me out. I began to doubt whether the hidden door existed. "

"Of course it does and why wouldn't I help you. You're my friend and besides Edward, Britney and Skylar are part of my family." Constance whispered.

"You sound troubled to me. What's going on?" Carly said.

"The ticking of Edward's life clock is slowing down. I didn't want to hear it but I did."

"What on earth does that mean?"

"Ghosts can hear the ticking of a being's life clock. It hasn't anything to do with their hearts. When the ticking slows down death draws near, but the person isn't immediately going to die. When the ticking becomes erratic and off beat, death is very near. I don't like to hear it but sometimes I do. Several times over the years, I've heard the slowing of a family member's life clock but couldn't do anything about it." Constance said.

"Should I warn Skylar?"

"I don't know. This has to do with the spirit world. I'm not sure Skylar can do anything about it, but if you want to do so go ahead." Constance said.

"I will and thanks. Does anyone else have a problem?"

"Not that I know of. Actually, I'm glad you're telling Skylar. I would like to help if I can." Constance said.

"Constance before you go, have you decided whether you will come to Tanglewood or not." Carly asked.

"Yes, I've thought about it a lot. I'm scared but I will come to the school if you promise to spend time with me. I don't want to be alone anymore." Constance said.

"Great news! I'll introduce you to my friends. Will become the Fab Five instead of the Fab Four. I may need your help convincing them you're real, but I think they'll like you just as I do." Carly said with some excitement.

"I sure hope so. Now I have to be off. I want to rest as much as I can before I go to Tanglewood." Constance said.

Carly felt Constance leave and joined the Worthington family and her friends who carefully inspected the hidden rooms. As she suspected, they loved the ornate library and study the most. Edward said he intended to immediately restore it and spend time there. Carly took Skylar aside just after they left the hidden rooms.

"Constance told me that your dad's life clock is slowing down. She says this happens when someone nears death, but isn't going to die immediately. There is a different sound for that. I'm sorry. Maybe you can persuade him to see a doctor."

"Unfortunately, this doesn't come as a big surprise. Dad has had a bad heart for a long time. He sees a heart specialist every few months. I try not to think about it, but I appreciate Constance trying to help. Can you can ask her to tell me if his life clock changes to that other sound." Skylar said.

"I'm sure Constance will tell me immediately if she senses any change. She considers you family." Carly answered.

"Funny I feel the same way about her. I never thought I would say that about a ghost let alone admit that there could be one." Skylar said.

Tanglewood

The Fab Four slowly settled into their routine at Tanglewood. They all studied very hard, pushing each other to do well. The Fab Four also tried to participate in all the school activities they could as well as play sports. The group felt so tired many nights they fell asleep at their computers or with a book in their hands. They seemed to be the perfect Tanglewood students well respected by both the teachers and the other students. Skylar even planned on running for class secretary at the end of the year. She was too young to run for president. Over the years, most Worthington girls held one of these elected positions at the school.

Still, adjusting to the clothing rules proved to be very difficult for them. Every girl had to wear a special Tanglewood Blue Blouse and Skirt. The blouse buttoned up to a girl's chin and the skirt hung down almost to a girl's ankle. None of the girls liked the outfit, but Jade liked it least of all. After wearing the outfit for a while, Jade's deep sea green eyes flashed with indignation as she told her friends how she felt.

"I hate this outfit! I couldn't attract a teenage boy with pimples all over his face in this. I have a pair of clothing scissors in my large make up case. What I ought to do is use it to cut this skirt short enough to become a mini-skirt. They're back in fashion you know. Then I can cut off half of the blouse buttons and wear a lacy black bra underneath. Then maybe I can give the boys I'm after something to look at. The outfit still won't be great but at least it will have a little fashion and sex appeal to it."

"Come on Jade, if you do that the headmistress will kick you out of the school. The reason they give us these ugly outfits and make us wear them is that they don't want girls to get in fights over their outfits. We had more than a few of those in my Junior High. Trudy the girl bully in my class told me that if I wore my tight jeans again she would give me a permanent fat lip. Trudy weighs in at about 250 lbs. She wore balloon dresses and hated girls who fit nicely into jeans. To protect my face, I had to leave my tight jeans at home. Can you imagine how bad it would be here with 400 rich estrogen filled girls wearing designer outfits? We'd be eyeing each other's outfits and making snide comments all day. Fist fights would break out all over the place." Peggy said.

"Yeah, these outfits go all the way back to the 19th century. Constance says that they're pretty similar to the ones she had to wear, but in her day, girls were expected to button the top button around their neck. Can you imagine that! At least we can leave the top button unbuttoned and sometimes even the second one." Carly added.

"Is Constance around? You haven't mentioned her until now." Skylar asked.

"She came the first few days but became scared with all the girls and teachers walking around here. Despite my best efforts to persuade her to stay, she returned to your house. She promised to come back but hasn't yet. It's been six weeks. I miss her. Anyway we need her to help us explore for the keys. She knows the tunnels and how to get into them." Carly answered.

"Yeah I feel it is my duty as a Worthington to look for the keys. All my ancestors including Constance did. I need to do so too." Skylar said.

"I don't know when were supposed to do that. They work us like dogs here. We are only freshman, young ones at that but they already have us in college preparatory courses. I study three hours a night and can't even keep up. Then there is our gym teacher. She looks like she pumps iron all day and drills soldiers on the side. Her head looks like it is directly attached to her shoulder. She always smells of stale sweat. If she keeps forcing us to pump iron and run like Jack Rabbits, I'll have bulging thighs and calves when I put on my bathing suit next summer." Jade complained.

"Jade I wouldn't worry about it. The amount of exercise we get here isn't enough to produce bulging muscles unless you're into steroids. Think of it as a way to keep our weight down and to look fit in a bathing suit. After being cooped up in here most of the year, I'm going to be spending my summer at the beach hunting for guys." Peggy said.

"I'll be right there with you." Jade added.

"We're all tired but the Fab Four still needs to pursue the keys. It's part of our mission as Tanglewood students. But, without Constance's help we aren't going anywhere. Skylar, I may need to go to your house for a few hours so I can convince Constance to come back to the school. Halloween is the best time to go looking for the keys and it is only two weeks away. Also, our big dance with Briar Manor is just before it. I think we can persuade Constance to spy on the Briar Manor boys. By doing that we can find out which girls they like. That will give us a big advantage. We won't have to waste our time chasing after the wrong boy." Carly said.

"Wow Carly I never thought of that. I plan on making a big play for Cory at the dance but he is a year and a half older than me. If he turns me down, I'll be crushed. Some intelligence from Constance would really help. Look, Carly, I told mom I'd be home Saturday night. You can come with me and spend the whole night trying to persuade Constance to come. Peggy, you and Jade can come too." Skylar said with some excitement as she paced around the room she shared with Carly. Peggy and Jade shared the door room next door.

"I can't come. I have to spend the whole weekend studying for an Algebra test. Math is hard for me and I need to be prepared. " Jade said looking down at her feet.

"I can't either. My mom doesn't want me to leave the school grounds for short trips at least for the first year. I doubt I could persuade her and don't even want to try. The last thing I need to hear is another lecture on how fortunate I am to be able to attend this school." Peggy said with a look of disappointment on her face.

"I'm lucky my parents know Skylar's parents so well. They said I could go to Skylar's house any time I want as long as I don't have any classes." Carly added.

"Okay then, Carly and I will bring Constance back to school. She'll be our secret agent and maybe our guide to the tunnels underneath the school. I'm excited just thinking about it. Like the rest of you I've been studying like crazy and working out. I need, we need to have some fun." Skylar said bouncing on the souls of her feet.

Powerful Dream

That evening, Carly had a terrible dream unlike any one she had before. Carly wandered through the tunnels underneath Tanglewood. Constance walked with her, but she looked like a real person not a ghost. Constance constantly talked and walked with a quick step causing her long braids to bounce on her back.

"Carly welcome to my real life such as it was back then. Even in my day the tunnels looked creepy. I hated spiders and rats and that's what seemed to inhabit the tunnels. Still, I tried to ignore my fear and keep walking. I explored almost every inch of the tunnels, sometimes walking for hours. After a while, I located the approximate place of the Magic Keys, but I never found them. I could feel their power. Oh now that I have you in here, I have to go. I'll see you as ghost in the real world."

When Constance disappeared before Carly could say anything, the walls began to move slowly in and out. The dark grey colors turned red. Carly could hear screams and the loud beat of a heart. The heartbeat grew louder, the walls moved faster, and the screams became so loud they seemed to come from inside Carly's head. Carly could feel sweat forming on her brow, as the now horrid place grew very hot. Then a face appeared, a horrible snarling face Carly didn't recognize. The lips moved and a hissing sound came forth that formed into words.

"I've been here so long, I forgot how new blood and souls nurtured and fed me until that new girl arrived. I sense your soul and blood and that of your friends will be even sweeter. You and your friends will come to me and when you do I will make you mine. I'll feast as I never have before. I've let so many of you pass through here without taking anything. I'll never let that happen again. Enjoy what you have for soon it will be mine."

The terrible face grew in size and its black mouth opened with sharp teeth dripping saliva all over Carly's face. Carly screamed from the very depths of her being then woke in her bed drenched in sweat. Carly somehow knew the identity of this terrible being in her dream. She had to be the evil-witch Elizabeth, reaching out to her from underneath the school.

Back to the House

Carly and Skylar sat next to each other on Skylar's king size bed. The room seemed very quiet, almost like a tomb. Skylar's purple passion perfume permeated the room. She complained.

"Where is Constance? Is she mad at us? We really need her help at the dance."

"I don't know. Every since I came into your house, I've tried to reach out for her but she isn't responding. I suppose we could try the Necromancer ceremony again. Wait a minute. Did you hear a cough?"

"No, I'm not a sensitive like you. She must be here listening to us. Talk to her."

"Okay Constance I know you're here. If you want to be our friend you need to speak." Carly said.

"I'm right next to you. I've been following you ever since you came into the house. I thought you would be mad at me for running away from the school. All those kids and teachers frightened me. I just didn't know what to say to you." Constance said right into Carly's ear.

"Skylar she just spoke to me. Constance is embarrassed she left the school. Constance thinks we're mad at her. I for one am not. Constance you're our friend and will stay our friend. It took a lot of courage to leave this house after 160 years. We just need you to come back to school for a few days."

"Constance my distant relative, I second what Carly just said. We really need your help at the Halloween dance. We don't want the Briar Manor boys telling us they like us when they really don't. We need you to listen to what they have to say about us and tell Carly so she can tell us." Skylar said.

"Wow you want me to be a spy. I can't think of anything else I would rather do. I used to read spy novels and murder mysteries all the time. Anyway, when it concerns teenage boys, we girls have to stick together." Carly said repeating what Constance told her. Carly continued. "From now on, I will repeat word for word what Constance tells me. It isn't right for me to interpret Constance. She needs to speak for herself."

"Thanks Carly. It's important for me to speak with Constance. She is my blood. I want her to be my friend and friends with the rest of the Fab Four too which we should really call the Fab Five now." Skylar said looking at a place she thought Constance might be.

"Skylar you don't know how much this means to me. Ever since I came back from Tanglewood, I've been thinking about going into the light because I disappointed you. Now I don't need to do so. I'm going to be a faithful member of the Fab Five. Not only will I spy for you but I will lead you into the tunnels under the school to look for the magic keys even though the tunnels really scare me." Carly said quoting Constance.

"Okay then distant cousin, you're officially a member of the Fab Five. Sit on the bed here and will plot our strategy for the dance. The Briar Manor boys won't know what hit them." Skylar said smiling at the empty space she thought Constance occupied.

"Wait a minute before we do that Constance I have to ask you a question. Last night I had a terrible dream where you led me into the tunnels underneath Tanglewood. An evil creature, which must have been Elizabeth the witch threatened to feed on my blood and soul. She said my friends and I would come to her. Were you in my dream last night?" Carly said. Carly as Constance answered.

"No, I wasn't. Anyway, I wouldn't do that. You're my friend. But as long as you girls are at Tanglewood, you're in Elizabeth's zone of power. I remember feeling that power when I lived at the school and have felt it the few times I returned to the school as a ghost. Elizabeth must have given you that dream."

"The dream still frightens me but I'm still determined to explore the tunnels underneath the school. No old witch is going to intimidate me. Anyway, let's return to more pleasant things: how we're going to snag some boys at the dance." Carly said her good mood returning.

Halloween Dance

The Fab Four spent almost two hours each trying to decide what outfit to wear for the Halloween dance, which actually took place a few days before Halloween. At the dances, they didn't have to wear their uniforms but they still had restrictions as to how much skin they could show and how short their skirts or dresses could be.

Jade who had been thinking about the restrictions for over a month found some partially transparent material she made into an otherwise conservative skirt and blouse. If you looked at the skirt and blouse in a certain way, a person could see the outlines of Jade's underwear underneath. Jade planned on showing the dress to the chaperones in a light that wouldn't reveal anything but allow the boys she liked to see the shadows of her underwear underneath. Jade spent hours practicing how to show the skirt and blouse to reveal what she wanted to reveal. Jade also wore her favorite blood red nail and toe polish. She had to put at least some color into her outfit.

Peggy adopted a different approach. She wore a medium length skirt and blouse covering her arms and her chest to her neck but left the two top buttons unbuttoned. Peggy selected a smaller size than normal for both the dress and blouse. In that way, her clothes clung to her body better showing off her curves. She selected pink toe and nail polish, her favorite color.

Carly chose a conservative but pretty dress. If the right guy danced with her, she could swirl the dress to show more of her legs than the rules would ordinarily permit. Carly also had Jade paint her toenails and fingernails with her blood red polish. She had to make some kind of statement.

Finally, Skylar selected a contoured dress with a long string of pearls, which a distant relative wore in the 1920's. Skylar even found the hat to go with it. Skylar wore her favorite nail and toenail polish, Ranch Red. She planned on using her best hip movement technique if she found a boy to attract.

The girls all wore lipstick, various shades of red, and subtle blush and eye shadow. Each of the girls had their own perfume, including the purple passion Skylar always wore. Peggy commented on Jade's Racy Red Mama, which came in a sparkling red perfume bottle.

"Jade I can smell you a mile away. You want to gently seduce a guy, not knock him off his feet with that powerful smell."

"Peggy you know me. I have to make a statement. And what is with that Jasmine stuff you have on. Its far too subtle for you." Jade replied.

"At least I don't have on roses like Carly. My grandmother wears rose perfume." Peggy replied.

"I don't really care what you girls think of my perfume. I like roses. It's the only perfume I can wear that doesn't make me feel sick." Carly responded holding her chin up.

"Okay enough back biting. We're the Fab Four or Five. Now let's help each other put on our makeup. We have only one shot at these boys. Let's make it count." Skylar said.

They all took turns applying each other's makeup. Carly, who had forgotten the comments about her perfume, suddenly spoke again to the other girls who ran back and forth to each other's dorm rooms.

"Constance is here. She is watching each of us get dressed. Do you want me to repeat what she says?"

"Absolutely as we all agreed we are now the Fab Five." Skylar said.

"What I think you girls need are some brightly colored silk scarves. Skylar has the long beads but the rest of you don't have anything on your front to catch the eye. I know where some scarves are located in Skylar's house if you don't have any." Carly said speaking for Constance.

"Great idea! I need something like that." Peggy said jumping up and down.

"Yeah, I just happen to have one in my luggage. I think the colors will match. Nothing in the rules says you can't wear one." Jade said as she quickly pulled out her suitcase and began to look through it.

"It just so happens I have some of the scarves you mentioned in my drawers. As you can tell, I like the retro look. Carly and Peggy do you have scarves or do you want to borrow mine? Carly with that dress on you really need some color and style." Skylar said.

"Sure, if you have a scarf that will work, I'd love to try it." Carly said.

"Yeah me too." Peggy commented.

"As a matter of fact, I think I have scarves that will work for both of you. Thanks Constance, I appreciate your advice. I only wish you could be with us for real." Skylar said.

"I do too but this is still a lot of fun for me. I can't wait to spy on the boys for you." Carly said for Constance.

Several hours later, the Fab Four stood on one side of the brightly decorated party room waiting for the Briar Manor boys. Someone burned incense sticks to hide the smell of the cleaning fluid they had used to polish the linoleum floor. Music played from the big old speakers lined up against the wall but the music had to be kept fairly low to prevent the speakers from making a vibrating noise. The girls made it past the chaperones without any trouble but the chaperones did stare at their scarves. Jade kept checking to see whether anyone could see her underwear. She finally decided to stand against the wall so no one could stare at her from behind. The rest of the girls made small talk and paced nervously back and forth. Then all of a sudden boys, dressed in neat sport coats and open dress shirts started to enter the room. All the girls wanted to stare but instead they tried to steal glances. Jades' eyes flew wide open when Thad strode into the room. She nervously addressed the other girls.

"What is he doing here? I didn't know Thad attended Briar Manor. He comes from a middle class family and attended public high school last year. I know he did."

"You forget he is a great football player. Briar Manor must have given him a scholarship." Skylar said.

"That's probably true but regardless he's here. I think I'm going to have a heart attack looking at him. I can barely breath. No boy should look that good." Jade said as she began to pace back and forth.

"Calm down Jade. I don't know what boys he is talking to but they look pretty cute too. Constance is walking over there to listen. Let's see what she learns." Carly said.

Several minutes later, Carly, Peggy and Skylar still nervously examined each boy that walked into the party. A very tall handsome chocolate skinned boy walked into the party. Peggy stared at him much the same way Jade stared at Thad. Finally she whispered to her friends.

"Oh my God is he gorgeous! Look he is walking up to Thad. I bet he is some kind of athlete. I think he glanced at me."

"Yeah he is another hunk for sure. I just wish someone like Peter would walk in here. I see a couple of interesting guys but no one I want to pursue." Carly said slowly.

Another several minutes passed. The music became more dance-oriented and some of the boys began turning their attention to the girls lined up with the Fab Four. At just this moment, Cory walked into the room with Peter at his side. Skylar stared at Cory and Carly stared at Peter. Carly spoke again.

"Does every boy we know go to Briar Manor? I know for sure that Peter attended the public high school. I can't believe it. Cory and Peter are walking up to Thad. All the boys we want are in one place. They are forming a group and talking to each other."

"5 O'Clock--there are some boys heading in our direction. They're swaggering but they don't have a whole lot to show off. They're definitely not what I'm looking for. Come on girls let's make ourselves scarce. I don't want to dance with a guy I don't like or have to say no to one of those guys if he gets up the courage to ask me. Also, I don't want Cory to think I'm taken." Skylar said as she began walking toward the other end of the room. The other members of the Fab Four followed Skylar. Skylar noticed Cory watching her as she left. When the girls found a spot in the back, Carly excitedly said.

"Our spy is back! I'll repeat what Constance says."

"The four boys you like noticed you looking at them. They think you're the most beautiful girls here, real babes as Thad put it. Surprisingly enough, as best I could tell, the boys you like seem to like you as well. Rufus, the handsome tall Negro or African American as you now call them, began laughing when the four guys headed toward you and you as a group left. Peter worried about your age. He said that you were only thirteen while they were fifteen. Anyway, if you like these guys,

I suggest you walk over to them. I saw another group of girls moving toward them. They're older and swaying their hips. "

"Hey we'll all be fourteen within a month. Those guys aren't that much older. I for one am headed over there right now. No other girl is going to move in on my territory. If I don't dance with Rufus, I'm going to be beating myself up all night for not having done so." Peggy said as she took off for the place the boys stood. Jade walked right behind her, followed by Skylar and Carly. When Jade reached the boys just ahead of the other group of girls Constance mentioned, she boldly addressed them.

"Welcome to Tanglewood. I'm Jade, this is Carly, Skylar and Peggy. If all of us weren't stuck in this ridiculous situation where we attend school only with our own sex, each of us would try to get to know you. Then leave hints as to which of you we wanted to date. But this meat market doesn't allow us to do that. We have to say what we mean without any delay. So here it is. I want to dance with you Thad; Carly wants to dance with you Peter; Skylar wants to dance with you Cory and Peggy wants to dance with you Rufus. Well what do you think?"

"Yeah okay. None of us are very good dancers but we came to a dance so that is what we should do. What do you guys think?" Thad said.

"I'm in." Peter said.

"So am I." Cory added.

"And me, but how on earth did you know my name? I'm not from here. I just transferred to the school." Rufus said with a puzzled look on his face.

"Believe me, girls have ways of finding these things out. Now let's go." Peggy said grabbing Rufus' hand.

Once the four couples began to dance, they barely noticed the time. They danced fast, slowly, seductively and any other way couples could dance. The perfume each of The Fab Four wore seemed to blend in the air with the boys' cologne. While the boys with the exception of Rufus danced poorly, their partners didn't mind nor care. Many times other boys tried to break in on Rufus, Peter, Cory, and Thad but the girls refused to dance with anyone else. When the music finally stopped, the four couples barely noticed. They just stood close to each other, dancing if the music still played. Finally, when the announcement went out over the loudspeakers that the bus to Briar Manor would soon depart, the couples broke apart. All eight of them gathered together. For the first time in hours, the boys spoke in complete sentences. Thad spoke first still staring in Jade's eyes.

"Um we have to go back. I don't know about the rest of the guys, but I had a great time. Let's exchange e-mails and cell numbers. We need to keep in touch."

"Thad we need to do more than that. We need to see each other that is if all of you want to be with us." Jade said.

"Of course I do Jade and I think the rest of the guys do too. I'm sure we'll figure something out." Thad said awkwardly.

"Oh come on you guys. We're into each other. That's the way it is. I don't really care what anyone thinks or says. Rufus you big handsome devil come here so I can kiss you." Peggy said also staring in her man's eyes.

Without another word said, the four girls reached up and kissed their boy. The boys kissed them back. They continued to kiss until one of the chaperones approached them.

"Ahem we don't allow that kind of thing at our dances. It's time for the boys to go back. At the very least, you could have found a more private place to do that. "

Skylar pulling back from Cory as did the rest of the Fab Four dreamily replied.

"Okay but don't expect us to feel ashamed for kissing the boys we danced with all night. Our parents lock all of us up in this place and Briar Manor for three quarters of the year. We have to be teenagers when we have the chance."

The chaperone shook his head and walked away. The four couples put their arms around each other and headed for the main entrance to Tanglewood. They spoke softly to one another and laughed. As the boys broke free, the girls quickly kissed them on the lips again. Within minutes the boys boarded the bus and the bus left for Briar Manor.

A half hour later, the girls walked back and forth between their adjacent dorm rooms. Carly who had been strangely quiet most of the evening spoke when the Fab Four gathered in her room.

"The whole evening seemed like a romantic dream to me. As I think about it, what are the chances each of us would be with a boy we like and have them like us back? It seems almost impossible. I had a couple of decent looking guys try to cut in on Peter and I but they just seemed like an annoying interruption. Even if the best looking guy in the world wanted to cut in, I wouldn't have let him. I knew of Peter before but tonight is the first time I actually spoke to him. Now look at me. I'm only thirteen going on fourteen and am already in love with a guy."

"It's the same for me. I feel like I'm floating on a cloud. All night I'm going be dreaming of Rufus. I just hope he's a good guy and doesn't have other women on the side." Peggy added.

"That makes three of us. I've been attracted to Cory for a long time, but I never spent any romantic time with him until tonight. My hormones really kicked in. My heart pounded. I had to struggle for breath. I just wanted to hold on to him forever and never let him go." Skylar said looking past her friends toward the ceiling.

"I'm in love too, but I worry that we came on too strong to our guys. I didn't even give Thad a chance to kiss me. I kissed him first. I also danced very close to him. I have to better control my desires." Jade said.

"Hah. This is 2014. What's wrong with us taking what we want? I'm not going to spend the next several months wondering what it is like to kiss Rufus. I already know." Peggy said lifting her chin a little.

"Ladies, Constance is constantly talking to me. I'm going to repeat a little of what she said." Carly continued as Constance. "Congratulations! In my day what happened tonight couldn't have happened for months. I hated waiting for my love to get in touch with me. By the time we finally did you what you did tonight, I already started to become sick. I wasted a lot of months when I could have been with my boyfriend. Oh and by the way, I heard those devices you carry chiming or whatever it is they do. Maybe your suitors are already trying to reach out to you. You might even have a love letter."

The four girls hurriedly pulled their smart phones out of their purses and checked their messages. All of them had a message from their dance partners. Carly spoke first.

"Peter needs a little practice in the wooing a girl category. He says he had a great time but he avoids saying anything about the way he feels. Still he did write. I haven't a clue as to what to say back to him."

"Thad must be getting his training from Peter. He said almost the same thing." Jade complained.

"Yeah that makes three of them. Rufus kind of stumbled over his words." Peggy added.

"Cory is a little better. He says I'm beautiful but like your guys says nothing about his feelings. If these guys are so careful about hiding their feelings maybe we should be the same way when we respond to their texts." Skylar said.

"Yeah, I don't want to get burned." Jade added.

The girls spent the next several hours, way beyond their lights-out-time, discussing what message they would send back to their suitors. Constance weighed in whenever she had the chance. Finally, the girls arrived at a format. They would say how handsome their boys were, but would not reveal any of their feelings. While they all wanted to jump in what they hoped would be their boyfriend's arms they didn't want to make fools out of themselves. They sent their texts, climbed into their beds and fell asleep.

Briar Manor

Rufus, Cory, Peter, and Thad, instead of playing catch at their lunch break, walked and talked on a fine seventy-degree day. Thad began the conversation.

"Jade is driving me crazy. I can't get her out of my head. She is so damn beautiful and sexy too. In ancient history class, the teacher talked about the Greek sirens, beautiful women who lured sailors into crashing on the rocks. Jade is just like those sirens. I'm worried she is going to burn me."

"In some ways, it's easier for me. I've known Skylar most of my life. Our families are close. We saw each other all the time at family events and at school too. Even though I was ahead of her in school, she always attended the same schools. By fifth grade, I already liked her even though she was still a little girl then. Now that she is a woman, I find myself very strongly attracted to her. She has always been so beautiful. Yet, in other ways, Skylar is hard to read sometimes. She seems like a character out of the Great Gatsby, which we just had to read for English: a beautiful rich girl in the 1920's. I never even knew she liked me until the Halloween dance. She didn't give me a clue. Still, I'm trying to keep my distance a little. I feel she could find some other guy and just walk away without giving the matter a second thought." Cory said.

"Cory you said almost everything I was going to say about Carly. Carly has always been the beautiful blond, even in grade school. You could tell how people reacted to her when she approached them. They always smiled and fawned all over her. I always thought she was out of my league and not only because of her beauty. She and Skylar are also very smart. They're always at the top of their class. When she started kissing me at the dance, I thought I would have a heart attack. Still, I don't know very much about Carly, but as Jade might do to you, Carly could easily break my heart. Like you Thad with Jade, Carly is in my head." Peter said.

"Wow this is a very strange conversation for four football players to be having. Remember we're supposed to be macho, the stars of the football team. We don't talk about girls this way. They come to us because we are the toughest and strongest males out there. We don't go chasing after them. Girls talk about relationships, we talk about sex." Rufus complained.

"Yeah I know, but that kind of male talk isn't going to help me figure out what to do with Jade. She is going to react very well to that kind of approach. As I already said, Jade has already stuck her beautiful long fingernails into me. So let me get this straight, Rufus. You're telling us that you don't care much about Peggy." Thad said with a little anger.

"No I didn't say that. Peggy is a real babe. She has all the right curves in the right places. She really knows how to kiss too. She just hasn't gotten her claws too deeply into me yet. Unlike you guys and your girls, I just met her. Still, I could see myself becoming like you romantic wrecks. Peggy could do that to me. Maybe you can tell me if that starts to happen. Then I can dump her. Someone here has to stand up for the football team." Rufus said with a strong voice as he paced in front of his friends.

"Rufus, as your quarterback, I'm telling you, you're farther gone than you think. Just like Thad said once they're in your head you can't just dump them. It's too hard. Anyway, let's get off this topic and throw the ball around a little." Cory said.

"We'll do that but first we have to deal with that twirp Chet. He is headed right for us. He thinks he's god's gift to women just because he sings so well and takes the lead in all the school plays. He really irritates me, but I guess we should listen to what the little runt says." Cory said.

Chet walked right up to the much larger Thad and immediately began to talk.

"Thad I know you were with Jade at the inter school dance. I've decided Jade is the most provocative, beautiful and interesting girl at Tanglewood, even though she is very young. I just wanted to let you know that I'm going to try and romance her. I figured it was better to just tell you up front rather than for you to find out later."

"Chet as a linebacker, I smash and hurt running backs and ends, but I do so as part of the game. It isn't personal. If you go after Jade, it's very personal to me. I'll squash you like a bug." Thad said turning red with anger as he towered over the much smaller Chet and clinched his fists.

Ignoring the threat, Chet responded with a little smile.

"You won't do that Thad. If you attack me, you'll lose your scholarship and probably have to leave the school. Even worse for you, a battered me will look like a very sympathetic guy to Jade, especially after I sing to her. You'll be helping me win the competition. Now I have to go. I have a short play practice before I have to start my next afternoon class. Oh and may the best man win. This is going to be fun." Chet said happily as he walked away from the four big guys who just stared at him. After a few minutes the shock finally wore off. Peter spoke first.

"Unfortunately Thad, Chet is right. You'll play into his hands if you beat him up. You're just going to have to pay a lot of attention to Jade so she ignores Chet. She already likes you. You have the advantage."

"Yeah maybe, but if he kisses Jade, I'll put him in the hospital even if I get kicked out of here. I won't be able to control my anger. Now in the few moments we have left before class, I'm going to go to the gym and hit the punching bag. I can pretend it's Chet's head. It's the only way I can calm down." Thad said as he turned and ran back toward the school just like he did on the football team.

"Thad really needs to get control of his anger.' Rufus said shaking his head.

"No Rufus he doesn't. That's what makes Thad a great linebacker. Maybe we ought to encourage Chet. If we do, Thad will beat up the other teams backs so badly they won't have a chance against us." Cory said.

"Yeah that would be good. Maybe these girls really are sirens. I can still feel Peggy's lips. That woman could wake up a half dead man. I've been trying not to think of her. Now thanks to you guys, she is going to be in my dreams tonight." Rufus complained.

"Join the club." Cory laughed.

Shopping

wo days after the dance, Jade threw up her hands and laid down on her bed her eyes fixed on the ceiling as the girls prepared for the morning meal and the classes that followed. As strong smells from their makeup and perfume filled the air, Jade, who had already applied her makeup and perfume complained loudly.

"I have shopitis, a serious condition. If I don't browse a clothing store soon, I'll curl up in a corner of my room and refuse to move. I need my fix!"

"That's a serious condition for a girl. I'm having a similar problem. I think having to wear these ugly school outfits is affecting all of us." Peggy added.

As usual, the four girls moved back and forth between their two adjacent rooms. Skylar turned to her friends and spoke earnestly.

"I've been thinking about a plan that might help. We have an hour and a half for lunch and tomorrow on Thursday all four of us have an hour study hall following lunch. After Mr. Simon takes attendance at study hall, he pays no attention to what we do until the bell rings. Debbie and I are slowly becoming good friends. I may ask her to join the Fab Four at some point. She offered to mark the four of us as present at the study hall when Mr. Simon isn't looking. At 80, Mr. Simon is easily distracted. He also forgets. The only thing he does is to check the attendance-list once he has marked it. So with Debbie's help we can slip out for two and a half hours tomorrow. I read the paper yesterday

"

and the day is supposed to be clear and relatively warm. As you know, the shopping mall is only a kilometer from where the main road meets the entrance to Tanglewood. So I propose we slip out after our last morning class and walk as fast as we can to the shopping mall. Then we can look at clothes which is what any self respecting teenage girl should be doing."

"Great but with the time we have we should be able to put on our new outfits and walk by the practice fields at Briar Manor, which are just down the road from the shopping center. Briar Manor eats lunch a half hour later than we do. I know the boys like to go to the practice field and play catch after they eat. If we hurry, we can walk by our boyfriends with our new outfits." Carly said with a great deal of excitement.

"What a great idea. You ladies are lifesavers. I don't even care if the teachers catch me. I've been dreaming about walking by Thad in a nice outfit. If I do, then I think I'll be cured of my disease." Jade said.

"Okay let's do it. Rufus, my man, Peggy is coming to see you." Peggy laughed.

The next morning, the Fab Four put on a little more makeup than usual. They also wore their favorite perfume. After applying a subtle lipstick, Skylar said.

"We have to be careful. If we put on too much makeup, the teachers might send us to the headmistresses' office. I saw them do it to, Rebecca the other day, but she kind of asked for it with white powder makeup and thick crimson lipstick."

"Why don't we put some hot lipstick and dark eyeliner in our bags? We can give our boyfriends the sexy look and then take the makeup off before we return to school." Jade said.

"I don't need to put that stuff on my face. If Peter doesn't like me without makeup, then he can get a new girlfriend. I like a little makeup but not that heavy stuff." Carly said.

"I'm with Carly. I may take some makeup along but I don't think I'll bring the heavy stuff. Some boys like makeup and some don't. I don't want Rufus to think I'm a lady of the night. Any way, let's go. I'm hungry and as you know if you go to breakfast too late, all the good food is gone." Peggy added.

Several hours later, like soldiers in a parade, the Fab Four marched out of the school. They left their books in their downstairs lockers. No one bothered them. Jade immediately started to complain.

"Come on girls walk faster. Every minute we spend traveling is one less minute we have to shop. I don't know where you girls are going but I'm headed straight for the Edge store. They have the coolest clothes. I persuaded my mom to take out a charge card that I can use there."

"My mother won't let me go to Edge. She says that only over sexed girls go to that store, whatever that means. I shop at Botany Bay. My mom said I could spend up to $200 a month there." Carly said.

"Botany Bay is okay with me. I like their retro clothing section. Anyway, my mother has a charge account I can use there." Skylar added.

"I guess that leaves you all alone Jade. My mom would kill me if she sees a bill from Edge. I'm going for Botany Bay too." Peggy added.

"You girls are making it tough on me. Would at least one of you check on how I'm doing with my selections?" Jade said with a distressed look on her face.

"We can do that. The two stores are right across from each other." Skylar said.

In near record time, the girls ran to the mall. They ran so fast, they even had to pause a moment to catch their breath. Only twenty minutes elapsed since they left the school. Jade without comment ran into Edge and headed for the skirt and dress section. Carly and Peggy headed for the same section in Botany Bay while Skylar ran to the vintage style section. Within ten minutes each of the girls had an armful of skirts and dresses to try.

"Ladies, thirty minutes of our two and a half hours is already gone. Don't come out of the dressing room if a dress or skirt doesn't feel or look right. It's a waste of time. For the ones you model, any of us out here will give you a rating from 1 to 10. Despite the rating, the final decision is with each girl. Okay?" Peggy said.

"Yeah that makes sense Peggy. I have two skirts and two dresses and I already pretty much have decided what I want." Carly said.

"Okay with me too but what about Jade?" Skylar said.

"You're not going to believe this but I just saw Jade run by the window in a very tight, short shiny deep blue skirt and head into Sheer." Peggy said.

"Lingerie? I should have guessed. She should have just gone there in the first place and ignored Edge." Carly said with a frown on her face.

"Come on Carly, don't be mean to Jade behind her back. Jade has it in her head that she has to be provocative to attract boys. She is very beautiful and doesn't need to do that, but she isn't going to listen to us say that anymore than she is going to listen to her parents. We just have to watch her very carefully and make sure she doesn't go too far. My big worry is that she is going to attract some aggressive men, the last thing girls our age need." Skylar said.

"I'm sorry I said that. The last thing I want to do is hurt Jade's feelings. This is a tough time for all of us being half women and half girls. Frankly I don't know what to wear most of the time. Even though I hate our school outfits, when I wear one I don't have to worry about having the right outfit. As to men, that's always a big worry of mine. When a man stares at me, it makes me feel creepy and uncomfortable." Carly said.

"Let's not think of that right now. We're wasting valuable time. It's time to try on our outfits." Peggy said.

The girls all nodded and quickly went into the dressing rooms.

A half hour later, Skylar selected a long sleeveless black dress, which fell below her knees but showed off her chest very well. Carly selected a shorter and looser blue dress with very little of her chest showing but unlike Skylar's dress Carly's dress had sleeves. Peggy selected a deep purple dress an inch shorter than Carly's that hugged her figure but did not show off her chest. Congratulating each other, Carly, Skylar and Peggy quickly left the store after paying.

"Ladies, I think we all deserve at least 9's, but I can't even begin to imagine what Jade picked." Peggy said.

"You don't have to imagine much longer, Jade is coming. My god, she looks like she is 25! She even put on that crimson lipstick." Skylar said with her mouth open.

Jade slinked up next to her friends with a wicked smile on her face. She had the short tight skirt Peggy saw earlier showing off her long lean legs but her matching blue blouse drew most of their attention. The blouse fit very tightly over her chest.

"How did you make your breasts look that way?" Peggy asked.

"A special kind of bra that's how. My sister wears one. Sheer had them so I bought one there." Jade declared.

"Okay but the three of us will surround you on the way out. We can't let any men see you like that." Skylar said with a little smile forming on her face.

"Very funny. I don't care if they see me or not. All I care about is that Thad sees me in this outfit. Speaking of that, we'd better hurry. More than an hour has already passed." Jade said.

"Okay we're off but we all thought you went in Sheer to buy some of their frilly underwear." Carly said.

"The saleswoman tried to persuade me to buy the matching panties but even I have my limits. My older sister might wear something like that but I never would. Let's put it this way, they don't use very much material in them, but charge a lot of money." Jade laughed.

"Jade that is why we love you so much. You're fun and a little bit outrageous, but I forgot to ask everyone, did you bring shoes to match your new outfits. As good as they look, the dirty tennis shoes we wear kind of wrecks everything." Skylar said.

"In my back pack." Peggy declared.

"In mine too." Jade added.

"I pulled them out three times to see how they matched my dress." Carly added.

"Of course I have mine too. Okay Fab Four, let's go hunt some boys. After they see us, they won't know what hit them. Oh and Jade, we're sorry we didn't give you comments on your skirt and blouse before you bought them. I'd give you a 10 but only because your using the outfit to attract Thad." Skylar said marching forward.

"It's okay. We didn't have much time. Anyway I got what I wanted and the high rating you just gave me makes me feel even better." Jade responded.

Arms around each other, giggling and laughing the girls almost ran toward Briar Manor. They reached the Briar Manor play field in front of the cafeteria fifteen minutes later. As luck would have it, Thad, Peter, Cory, and Rufus threw a football back and forth to each other. The girls ducked behind a tree and quickly changed their shoes. When they finished, Carly exclaimed a little too loudly.

"Jade, now those are truly high heels. How do you walk in them? I would sprain my ankle."

"Practice my dear, practice. Even so I may have to lean on you. This ground is a little rough for shoes like this. They are meant for flat smooth surfaces." Jade worried.

After they emerged from behind a tree, Peggy, always ready to say something, called to the boys running in front of them.

"Hey Rufus, do you have a moment to talk?"

As soon as Rufus turned, The Fab Four began to hip walk back and forth behind the metal fence. Rufus, smiling broadly, collected Thad, Peter and Cory and the four of them slowly walked to the fence. As they did, Thad flexed his biceps, Peter sucked in his stomach, Cory held his head high, and Rufus performed his super cool walk. While some of the other boys on the field noticed what happened, the teachers and administrative personnel who happened to be outside talked to each other and didn't notice the commotion.

As the four boys approached, they had different reactions. Thad just stared at Jade with his mouth open. Cory tried to look as sophisticated as possible as he stole side-glances at Skylar. Peter just smiled broadly as he carefully watched Carly. Rufus began to say something but before he could, Peggy spoke again.

"Well boys what do you think?"

"Babes you're putting it on. I've been thinking about you ever since the dance. You look even better today than you did then." Rufus said.

"Yeah Jade, you belong in some kind of beauty contest. I'm gong to have nightmares after seeing you like this. Well, not nightmares, I mean really good dreams." Thad said stumbling over his words.

Jade smiled but caught her shoe. Carly quickly prevented Jade from falling. Jade in an attempt to distract the boys from her near fall stared at Thad and said.

"I guess I need a strong man around to help me."

Peter jumped in.

"Carly you look really great in that dress. I almost forgot how beautiful you are. The only women we see here are the teachers and the secretaries, most of whom aren't very good looking."

"Okay that leaves me. Skylar what can I say. You always manage to look classy and sexy at the same time. You've always been the best-looking girl in our group of friends since grade school. I just feel lucky you like me." Cory said.

"If you boys really think we like you, you need to come to this side of the fence and find out. We had to slip out of school. We're running out of time." Skylar said with her sexiest voice.

The Briar Manor boys didn't need any more encouragement. They ran as fast as they could toward the place they could exit the field and take the road to where the girls waited. The Fab Four quickly slipped behind the large oak tree as they noticed one of the teachers turning toward them. As they hid on the other side of the large oak, Carly said with her eyes wide.

"What are we going to do when the boys get here?"

"I don't know about you but I'm grabbing Thad and kissing him. Thad isn't a great talker anyway, but he sure looks great." Jade said.

"That makes two of us. Just looking at Rufus has my heart beating so hard it is about to come out of my chest." Peggy sighed.

"I don't know. I kissed Peter at the dance so I guess I'll kiss him again, but I'm a little mad at all our so-called boyfriends. They should be taking risks like we are to see us not the other way around. They make it seem like we are stalking them and have no other choices than them." Carly complained.

"Welcome to our generation Carly. Chivalry is dead or at least dying. Still, it irritates me too that we have to go to all this trouble. If they think we're hot, they should be knocking down our door." Skylar added.

"Are you going to kiss Cory then? Jade asked.

"Yes, after all this trouble I feel I have to kiss him, but I don't know how passionate I will be." Skylar answered.

The boys arrived a few minutes later. Meanwhile the girls had taken off their shoes and put their sneakers on instead. They needed to move quickly when the time came. The moment the boys drew near, the Fab Four reached up and kissed their boyfriends but held back a little. Even Jade came to her man slowly. Jade suddenly felt as if she had to do all the work in her relationship with Thad. Letting go of Peggy, Rufus made the first comment.

"Hey that is not the kiss I remember from the dance. It was almost polite, like a kiss from a relative."

"Rufus all of us are a little annoyed that we had to take risks to come over here and see all of you. Boys are supposed to take these risks not girls. All I have gotten from you is some brief non-committal e-mails and texts. Even if you're cute, your romance score is near zero. If you don't know by now, romance is important to girls." Peggy replied.

"You girls are too impatient. We have a plan to visit you on Sunday Night Halloween. We had to make sure we had some friends we could trust to cover our escape." Peter said looking at his friends.

"Yeah we have some monster masks to scare you." Thad added.

"I'm not sure monster masks are romantic, but if you guys show up Halloween night, I for one will be kissing you Thad much more passionately than today." Jade said.

"The same for me," said Carly.

"And me," Skylar added.

"That makes all of us. Now we have to return to our school before they put us on probation and take away our privileges." Peggy said.

"Oh and boys or monsters if that is what you are, you have no idea how passionate the witches you find at Tanglewood will be on our most sacred night. We will permanently light your fire." Skylar said as she kissed Cory lightly on the lips and turned to walk back down the road.

The other three girls did the same thing to their boyfriends and joined Skylar. The Fab Four hip walked and waved to their boyfriends as they quickly moved away from Briar Manor. As the girls disappeared down the road, Cory complained.

"Peter you saved us, but we're going to have to make good on our promise to sneak out to see them on Halloween or kiss our girlfriends goodbye. As hot as they looked today, I certainly don't want to do that. I'm going to be seeing Skylar slink by in that dress all night in my dreams."

"It's all I could think of to say. All four of those girls are hot in their own way. Carly sure is. We couldn't lose them. Half the boys in the school are asking me how I scored with Carly. It would drive me crazy if she took up with someone else." Peter said.

"Those must be the same guys who are pestering me about Jade and of course there is that jerk Chet who keeps telling me he is after Jade. As to Jade, every night I go to sleep I see those magical green eyes of hers." Thad added.

"We have work to do then. We need a plan. Peggy is too fine to let go. I can still taste her red hot lips on my mouth." Rufus said.

Meanwhile the girls had their own conversation.

"Carly thanks for the save. Now we have the boys coming to us as they should. Although I must say, I wanted to kiss Thad harder." Jade said.

"We all wanted to kiss our boyfriends harder, but they have to earn it first. Anyway, I have a cool idea. If those boys are going to show up with monster masks, why don't we give them a real scare? I'll talk to Constance and see what she can do to freak them out." Carly said.

"That's a good idea but just don't freak them out too much. I wanted to kiss Rufus for at least ten minutes but I only kissed him for a few seconds. That is like having the appetizer and not the meal." Peggy said.

"Do you think they really planned on coming to see us?" Skylar asked.

"Probably not, but after seeing us today now they will. Remember we are the Fab Four or Five if you count Constance. We have to demand respect from our boyfriends or otherwise they will take us for granted. By the way, how much time do we have?" Carly answered.

"About thirty five minutes. Why don't we dash into Botany Bay and change. It's on the way. Then, if anyone sees us at Tanglewood, we'll have on our uniforms." Jade said.

"A good idea but let's hurry. I don't want to get detention and have to deal with an angry father and mother." Peggy added.

Thirty-five minutes later, as the Tanglewood girls left study hall, the Fab Four quietly slipped into the group next to Debbie. They all breathed heavily from running and had beads of sweat on their faces. Debbie winked and said.

"Skylar study hall has to be the most boring thing we do at this school."

"You're right about that Debbie. Even though I try to study, most of the time I end up looking at the ceiling." Skylar responded with a smile.

Halloween

The Fab Four dressed for the school's Halloween Party with their usual flair. Skylar wore a long black dress, reaching the floor. The dress surrounded the base of Skylar's neck. She had a black witches' hat and used thick layers of white make up and blood red lipstick on her face for contrast. She also wore a nice necklace of semi precious jewels and her tallest high heels. Skylar put on some perfume a relative gave her. Skylar kept the musty smelling perfume for events such as these. Skylar painted her nails and toenails with her blood red polish.

Jade dressed as a zombie with large amounts of white powder and black eye liner and a short tattered dress. Her hair usually carefully combed and shinny she teased into a raggedy mop. Her fingernails, usually perfect, she painted a dull brown. She placed her oldest and dirtiest sneakers on her feet. She rubbed some juice from a pear that had been out too long on her face as perfume.

Peggy, deciding to be a vampire, wore heavy white makeup, blood red lipstick, plastic fang teeth and a black satin robe. She also wore a huge fake ring of blood red glass and placed her feet in black high heels. Peggy rubbed some cheap perfume that smelled sickly sweet on her neck. She also wore Jade's blood red toe and nail polish.

Carly wore white sheets formed into a throw over dress tied at the waist with a white rope and white comfort shoes. Carly died her blond hair white and also placed white powder all over her face. Carly didn't wear perfume thinking that the white powder created the kind of smell she wanted. Carly also painted her nails and toenails white. None of them wore masks thinking that the ones they saw in the stores looked cheesy. Constance through Carly made the first comment.

"I guess Peggy is supposed to be a vampire but most of what I know of that is from what I have overheard people say as a ghost. As to Jade, she appears to be a corpse, although I must say I don't know very much about the way they look. I never looked at my dead body or anyone else's for that matter. Skylar makes a very good witch, I've always imagined Elizabeth looks like Skylar in her outfit, but I am not sure about Carly. Even though ghosts are always represented as being white, we really appear in the same variety of colors we did when we were alive. Yet, live people don't know that, so the outfit works. The other kids and the adults will know that you're a ghost. All and all, you've made a good effort."

"Yeah, we look okay but remember dressing for this boring school party is not our main goal here. We want to be with our boyfriends for as long as possible. To duck out of the school party, we have to look like we have dressed for Halloween. Also, we want you to really scare our boyfriends. They said they would scare us. You can change all that. What do you think you can do?" Skylar asked.

"All Saints Eve is a special time for ghosts but why I can't tell you. Any way, near midnight our power greatly increases. We can actually appear for a few seconds without any risk of going into the light. What I thought might be great is to appear to all eight of you, then do my changing into a skeleton act. The boys will be scared but won't want to admit that they are in front of their girlfriends. They will want to appear manly and above it all." Constance said through Carly.

"Great, I can't wait to see their faces! Boys are always pretending they are so tough. Tonight we will see just how tough they are." Peggy said with a gleam in her eye.

"Okay let's review our plan and make sure we know our part. When the time nears eight, we will gather in that part of the party room nearest to the hallway that leads to the back door. When Peter texts Carly, Skylar will leave the party and open the door. She will then take the boys to the library, which is always open but will be empty during the party. After a few minutes, each one of us will quietly leave the party and join our boyfriends. If anyone asks, Debbie, who covered for us on our shopping trip, will tell the proctors or teachers that we headed off to the bathroom to work on our outfits." Jade said, trying to summarize the plan.

"Jade I think you have it just right. Okay ladies, lets go to the party, drink some non alcoholic fruit punch, yuck, munch some cookies, and show all the girls in this place how good the Fab Four can look." Skylar said.

The girls worked the party for the first hour, examining each girl's outfit and making comments on some. The school asked them to vote for the outfits they liked best. The winners would be announced at the end of the party. Even though they thought their outfits were among the best, the Fab Four hoped none of them would be selected. They had other pressing business. The girls finally settled in their location near the back door hallway. The boys promised to text them when they arrived. They said they would be there at eight but the girls grew nervous as the old grandfather clock in the hall counted out eight rings.

"They better show or all they will get is my fist not my lips." Peggy said pacing a little.

"I'm not even sure I want Thad to see me like this. I don't look very sexy in this outfit." Jade complained.

"You're not supposed to look sexy. You're supposed to look dead or crazy or evil, something like that. I doubt our boyfriends will look that good either." Carly replied.

"If I'm not sexy I might as well be dead, but I guess that is what tonight is all about isn't it." Jade said with a slight smile.

"Peggy, I'm beginning to feel like you. I'm new to this dating thing but any boy meeting me or asking me out better be on time. It is a matter of respect." Skylar said.

"Yeah any boyfriend making me wait will be an ex boyfriend." Carly added.

Ten more minutes passed then suddenly Carly raised her hand.

"They're here and not to soon. The teachers look like they are going to hand out the costume awards. It'll be harder to escape then."

Skylar slipped out of the room and walked down the hall as quietly as she could. The other girls followed moments later.

The Fab Four carefully examined their boyfriends' outfits before they said anything. Thad wore a muscle shirt, jeans and heavy combat boots. A rubber troll mask covered his face. To complete his outfit,

Thad carried a hockey stick as a club. Jade didn't think much of the outfit but forced a smile anyway.

Rufus had on a store bought vampire outfit with the same plastic teeth as Peggy. Peggy felt the same way as Jade but also managed to smile at her man. His dirty sneakers peeked out from underneath the robe.

Peter wore a Frankenstein outfit, which included a mask and nobs sticking out of his neck. He wore heavy black work boots. Carly forced a smile as well. She would have to help Peter design a better outfit next Halloween if they remained girlfriend and boyfriend.

Finally, Cory wore a zombie mask and tattered clothing. He uttered appropriate zombie sounds and swung his arms at Skylar who laughed and moved away.

"Okay you guys came as we asked and dressed up for Halloween. Although I have to say, we liked you better in your football uniforms. Still, it's time for your reward." Jade said as she reached up, removed Thad's mask and kissed him as hard as she could.

The other three girls did the same thing with their boyfriends. For several minutes, the couples kissed and hugged each other. Then Constance whispered in Carly's ear.

"Are you ready for me yet?"

Carly slowly pushed away from Peter. Some of her white powder rubbed off on Peter's face. The other three girls pushed away from their boyfriends, Peggy doing so well after everyone else.

"That was great, ladies. Where to next, your dorm rooms?" Rufus asked, his eyes wide.

To everyone's surprise, Jade answered in an unexpected way.

"No the security is too tight here. Someone would find us. If they do, all of us would be facing detention maybe even expulsion. When my mother and father found out, they would kill me. We're already taking a great risk doing what we're doing. We could go outside but the night is cold. I'd freeze."

"Jade is right. My parents felt great pride that their only daughter attended an elite school like this one. It would break their hearts if the school expelled me for having a boy in my room. Anyway, going to our rooms is a little fast for me." Peggy added.

"Come on ladies. You asked us over here. Skylar you're a redhead. You don't just want to be a tease, do you?" Cory said.

Skylar turned toward Cory anger working its way into her voice." The color of my hair hasn't anything to do with the way I am."

Cory didn't know how to respond to Skylar. He had never seen her so angry. So he wisely fell silent. Thad, however, continued the conversation.

"Look they're other girls who wanted to be with us. We are after all the stars of the football team."

Carly sensed that the boys would keep turning up the pressure on all of them. She liked Peter but didn't want him in her bedroom. Carly whispered to Constance that the time had come. Then she announced to the group.

"Let's put off our discussion of you going to our rooms for a little while. I sense this rendezvous is not headed in the right direction. If you will all turn toward the door, we have a surprise for you. It's after all Halloween."

As the girls turned and the boys followed, Constance slowly began to materialize out of thin air. Carly knew what Constance looked like but the rest of the Fab Four didn't. When she finally assumed her form, hoop skit and long braids included, Constance spoke.

"Hi I'm Constance. I died in 1850, while I attended this school. These girls are my friends. I appeared to celebrate Halloween the most sacred holiday for a ghost. Oh and to scare you. Boo."

With that statement, Constance slowly changed into a skeleton, cackling as she did so. With her skeleton jaws moving, Constance suddenly disappeared. Thad broke the long silence that followed with a nervous laugh.

"That looked real. I don't see any projectors in here."

"Oh that's Constance. She is a real ghost and a distant cousin of mine. We talk to her all the time through Carly who can see and hear her most of the time, but ordinarily we can't. Because it's Halloween night, Constance is very strong. She saved up all her energy to appear before us. She wanted to give us a special treat." Skylar said.

"This is kind of freaky. We sneaked out of Briar Manor to be with you, but we didn't expect to see a real ghost. Just like you, I'm beginning to worry we might get caught. The proctor will be checking our rooms in about a half hour. I don't think the pillows in our beds are going to fool him. He probably did the same thing at Briar Manor when he attended. Why don't we see you girls later." Peter said nervously as he began to pace.

"Yeah our Halloween party is over. It's a good time for us to return." Rufus added.

"Okay guys, we'll have to plan our next get together so we can spend so more quality time with each other. Maybe we can find a better and more intimate place. Should we ask Constance to come along?" Skylar said.

"No that's okay. Constance can stay right here. We don't need her spying on us." Cory added.

"Sorry about that. We wanted to do something special for you. You promised to scare us. We tried to do the same." Carly said.

"No ghost is going to scare me, but like Peter I think we need to get out of here." Rufus added. As the boys turned to go, Jade reached up and kissed Thad.

"This turned out to be too quick, but we really enjoyed seeing you guys."

The other three girls grabbed and kissed their boyfriends goodbye as well, but the boys did not linger as they had the first time. In a matter of moments, they left the library and exited the back door without saying goodbye. Jade spoke first.

"Constance saved us. Thad hugged me so hard I couldn't breathe. All this talk about going to our rooms upset me."

"Me too. Rufus kissed me so hard my lips hurt." Peggy added.

"I had a similar experience. These boys need to learn that girls don't play football." Carly said with her arms folded on her chest.

"Cory started out alright then he started to bear hug me. If he wants to date a girl wrestler he ought to do that." Skylar complained.

"I'm worried they will cut us off. Remember your boyfriend Cory called us teases." Jade said.

"If that is all they want from us, we are better off without them." Carly said stomping her feet.

"I don't know. Despite him coming on a little strong, I still like Rufus." Peggy said looking at her feet.

"I think we all still like our boyfriends. We just have to set some limits." Skylar said.

The girls all nodded then Carly said.

"Ladies before we return to the party, Constance wants to know whether her performance worked. In all her time as a ghost, she has never appeared that long and been able to speak as well. She thinks it's because of Halloween but she also felt a surge of energy coming from below the school."

"I wonder if the energy surge has something to do with the magic keys and the witches. They're supposed to be down there somewhere. As to Constance's appearance, I thought it was great and agree with Jade that it saved us. Our boyfriends had one idea about what would happen tonight and we had another. Constance appearing as she did took their attention away from what they wanted to do." Skylar answered.

"I agree. We have to be smarter about this dating thing in the future, especially when we date older boys. It's going to take me a few days to sort out all my conflicting emotions, but at least now I have time to do it." Peggy added.

"I know what you mean Peggy. I like being provocative and sexy like my older sister but then when I am with a boy I feel like a scared little girl at my first fifth grade dance. Attracting boys is the easy and fun part but what to do with them once they are with you is difficult." Jade said.

"Exactly Jade, exactly." Carly said.

As the girls returned to the party, Debbie came running up to them.

"Thank goodness, you're back. Skylar just won the best natural girl costume award. When you didn't show, Skylar, the headmistress sent some girls to find you. I told the headmistress that all four of you headed to the bathroom. I'd walk up to the front right now before this starts to look bad. What are you going to tell them?"

"That we were in the library talking after leaving the bathroom. Since this is mostly true, the teachers and headmistress should believe us. Did I really win the award?" Skylar said.

"Yes, now get moving before all of us get in trouble." Debbie said.

Field Hockey

The Fab Four all tried out for and made the junior varsity field hockey team. Skylar excelled in junior high and received a spot on the starting team. Carly and Jade spent most of their time on the bench but occasionally substituted for a tired or hurt starting player. Peggy hadn't played before coming to the school but already earned a starting position. While her stick play needed some improvement her blazing speed caused problems for opposing teams. On several occasions, she would suddenly turn up in front of an opposing team's goal even though the defense made every effort to stop her. These almost free shots would occasionally go in the goal, helping Tanglewood win some close games they might not have otherwise won. Skylar talked Peggy, Carly and Jade into trying out for the team. As members of the Fab Four, they all felt they had to join.

Today they faced the undefeated Pinewood Manor, the best junior varsity hockey team in the conference. They also had the best varsity team. Indeed many of their junior varsity players would have qualified for other teams' varsities. Through very hard play and with a little good luck, Tanglewood managed to tie Pinewood Manor after a Peggy breakaway late in the last period. Peggy's shot took a funny bounce and dribbled passed the Pinewood goalie, who seemed at first to have stopped it. At a break, Peggy and Skylar sat down next to Carly and Jade. Skylar complained loudly.

"Betty the bomber is killing me. She is like our coach Matilda. The girl is all muscle with her head barely peeking out of her shoulders. She has hit my legs so many times with her stick I look like I have black and blue disease on my legs. I can't let Cory see me like this. I'll have to wear stockings the next time I see him."

"Sister I know what you mean. Betty is constantly trying to trip me or push me out of the way. They don't call the penalties against her that they should. Anyway, I've got an idea Skylar. When I get the ball in the center, instead of passing it to you as I usually do, I want you to run right at Betty. I'll follow behind you and dart off to the left at the last minute. With you in front, I should be able to get to the goal without her stopping me as she usually does. The other defensemen will move to intercept but it will be too late. What do you think?" Peggy said.

"Sounds good to me Peggy. She'll give me a stick to the legs, but she'd do that anyway. Let's see if it works." Skylar responded.

"Good luck ladies. Remember, you're part of the Fab Four. Make us proud. We've done our part. It's up to the starters like you to finish the game. I'd really like to stick my nose up at that cow Betty and the rest of that team that thinks they are god's gift to field hockey." Carly said.

"Yeah that goes for me too--Fab Four forever." Jade added.

Peggy and Skylar waved at their friends and took up their positions. They're opportunity came three minutes later. Skylar intercepted a weak pass from a Pinewood defense girl. Skylar headed for Betty who moved to intercept her. At the last moment, Skylar hit the ball back to Peggy and kept running toward Betty. Betty whacked Skylar with her stick to push her out of the way, but Peggy easily moved passed Betty, who struggled to move past Skylar. As Peggy approached the goal with the other defense girls trying to intercept, Peggy hit a slap shot toward the goal that she hit just right. The ball sailed into the net.

The girls gathered around Peggy hugging and patting her on the back. When she moved free of her teammates, an angry Betty the bomber stepped in front of her. Skylar immediately moved to Peggy's side. Betty bellowed.

"Skylar you interfered with me. Peggy would never have made that breakaway otherwise."

"Yeah and you tripped me Betty like you always do. You're just sore because we scored on you with only a minute left and as a result you'll probably lose this game." Skylar challenged.

"The only reason you scored any goals was that you put this ringer on your team. Everyone knows they run faster than normal people. People like her play basketball or run track, they don't play a white game like this." Betty responded.

Skylar turned a bright shade of red, her temper flaring.

"What! How dare you insult my friend that way, you tub! I'll tear your eyes out."

"Nobody calls me a tub, especially not a runt like you." Betty said as she pushed Skylar to the ground.

Enraged, Skylar quickly gained her feet and jumped at the much larger and stronger Betty, pushing her to the ground. Peggy jumped on as well before Betty could destroy Skylar with a roundhouse right. Several of the Pinewood players tried to pull Skylar and Peggy off Betty. More Tanglewood players joined in the fight. Carly and Jade immediately got to their feet. Jade said.

"Our sisters are in trouble. Let's go."

"I'm with you." Carly replied as she started running toward the pile. Despite Matilda yelling at them to stop, Carly and Jade jumped on the pile, tearing a Pinewood girl off Peggy before she could scratch Peggy's face. They also grabbed Betty's arm before she could throw a devastating punch at Skylar's head. Minutes later, several big adults including Matilda removed all the girls from the pile and separated them on the field. The fight ended, as did the game.

Later that day, the Fab Four, covered with scratches and a few bandages, walked into Tabatha's, the headmistresses' office. Tabatha just stared at the girls as they sat down. She started speaking with a heavy sigh.

"Skylar you're one of the leaders in this school, just as your ancestors have been. The other girls look up to you. The same could be said of the rest of you girls. Why did you foolishly attack the player from the other team, Betty I think her name is? You had to know there would be consequences."

"Betty insulted my friend Peggy. She called her racial names. No one does that to my friend and gets away with it. In American History class, the teacher praised the white people who stood with African Americans during segregation. I'm no different than them. As long as they're people like Betty someone has to stand up to them, no matter the consequences." Skylar replied.

"And the rest of you girls, do you feel the same way."

"When Betty said all those racial things to me, I was too shocked to respond. Skylar like the good friend she is did. When I came to my senses, I joined in the fight which was my fight.in the first place." Peggy said.

"We didn't hear what Betty said, but our friends we're in trouble. So we went to their rescue. If I had, I'd have punched that cow in the mouth." Carly said with anger in her voice.

"Me too," Jade said nodding her head.

"Girls, violence is never the answer to anything. For that reason, I must discipline all of you. Still, from the eyewitnesses, I know Betty started this fight. Also, I admire you girls standing up for your friends and against racial discrimination, which is very strongly condemned by this school. So, I'm going to put you on probation for a week. Any serious problems that occur during this time will result in a one-month suspension. Also, you girls will be unable to play on the field hockey team for the remainder of the year, not that this makes any difference. So many of your fellow teammates will receive the same punishment, we will have to forfeit the rest of the season. It's too bad. You qualified for the playoffs. If it's any consolation, Pinewood is also forfeiting the remainder of its games. I hope this teaches all of you a lesson." Tabatha said.

"We accept your punishment, but we'll never apologize for doing what we think is right." Skylar said. The other girls nodded their heads in agreement.

"Okay you girls better leave before I decide to increase your punishment", Tabatha said as she waved the girls away.

Football Game

The Fab Four slowly recovered from their field hockey incident. They easily lasted through their one-week probation and started to put the field hockey season out of their mind even though they were convinced they would have won the championship. With more time on their hands, the girls began to focus on their boyfriends. They continued to text and e-mail them, but they had yet to find a place for their next more intimate meeting. Jade heard rumors that Thad and Rita a junior at Tanglewood spent some time with each other. Jade asked Thad about it, but he hadn't responded to her question. She interpreted this as Thad admitting to the relationship. Jade complained bitterly to her friends.

"I just got together with Thad and he is already cheating on me. Do you think it's about us not wanting the boys to come up to our rooms?"

"Yeah probably that and maybe Constance appearing had something to do with it. I don't know. What I do know is that relationships are very difficult. We just have to keep looking for the boys who work for us. Peter hasn't been very communicative to me either. He writes one-sentence responses to my e-mails. I wouldn't be surprised if he hooked up with another girl. They may have all started dating someone else." Carly responded.

"I haven't given up that easily. Jade isn't so easy to dismiss. If this tryout for cheerleading works, I have a plan to restart Thad's interest in me." Jade said.

"This isn't going to be very easy for you. Both Carly and I did a little cheerleading in middle school. You and Skylar didn't. Because this is a trial run for one game to see if Tanglewood cheerleaders will work at Briar Manor games, I heard that the athletic director is thinking about just using girls with experience. You may just have to go as a spectator. Next year if we cheerlead for all of Briar Manor's football games, they will have longer tryouts. You'll have a better chance of making the squad then." Peggy said.

"We'd have a better chance if they didn't have boy cheerleaders taking up all the spots. Honestly, I think the Briar Manor boys would much rather see us than their classmates doing splits and tumbles." Skylar complained.

"Skylar, you and Jade may still have a chance. I heard that they might appoint some alternates to perform if a girl becomes sick or injured. The alternates will be allowed to wear the cheerleading outfits and stay on the sideline in case they are needed. You ladies can concentrate on performing for Cory and Thad while we do the actual work expected of cheerleaders." Carly said.

"Sounds great! I hope you're right and I make the alternate squad. My plan will work then." Jade responded.

A week later the Fab Four headed for Briar Manor's final football game against Winston last year's private school champions in a rickety old school bus that misfired with loud bangs. Carly and Peggy made the cheerleading squad and Skylar and Jade made the alternate list. They all had their cheerleading outfits on under their warm coats. Peggy complained.

"I'm going to freeze my butt off in this cold. I'm a southern girl. I don't look good with goose bumps."

"I'll do the first routine and rush back to the bench and put my coat back on. I'm not going to stand there with my knees knocking waiting for the next routine." Carly added.

"Stop complaining, at least you can perform for Rufus and Peter. We have to sit there and watch." Skylar said with some unease.

"Skylar, you need a plan like me to get your boyfriend's attention. I'm not going to tell you what it is, but it's going to work. I know it will." Jade added.

"Hmm, you didn't make lunch Wednesday, which is not like you. You eat more than all of us put together. You're the only girl I know who can eat whatever she wants and not gain an ounce. I wonder where you might have gone." Peggy said.

"My stomach bothered me. I didn't feel like eating. I stayed up in my room." Jade said.

"Funny, I saw you wolfing down some snacks just after lunch. I'll tell you what I think Jade. You sneaked off to Sheer at lunch didn't you." Carly said.

"Maybe, but so what. I needed a few things." Jade answered slowly.

"No, you didn't Jade? You told us you wouldn't buy those racy panties." Skylar said with shock on her face.

"I didn't. I found some the same size and fit as my normal underwear but with the frills and the black silk." Jade said with her chin lifted.

"You don't have those on now, do you?" Peggy asked.

"I do, but it's really no big deal. I'm an alternate. No one is going to see my underwear except Thad. If I can persuade him to meet me under the bleachers, I'll do my cheerleading routine for him and him alone. There you have it. Now you know my plan." Jade said.

"And if you are asked to substitute for a missing girl. What then? Are you going to show everyone in both schools your Sheer panties?" Carly asked.

"Of course not. Skylar can fill in for the missing girl." Jade responded.

"You better hope only one cheerleader can't perform. Otherwise, you're in big trouble." Skylar said.

"It's worth the risk. I'm not going to let Thad throw me away for some older girl." Jade said with determination on her face.

An hour later, Peggy and Carly warmed up on the sidelines. Peggy could really fly. She jumped higher and faster than everyone, but she saved her biggest split for Rufus when he ran on the field. Rufus pretended not to notice but did turn his head toward Peggy. Carly didn't have Peggy's spring but she did her cheerleading routines very well.

The Briar Manor cheerleaders, who would perform every other cheer, started their routines after the girls finished. As Jade and Skylar watched, they found themselves impressed with their jumping and tumbling ability. Although not big and muscular like the football players, the girls decided several appeared to be quite handsome. Preoccupied with the male cheerleaders, Jade didn't notice that Matilda, the head of the Tanglewood sports program and of course their field hockey team couch stood in front of her.

"Jade and Skylar, you should warm up with the other girls. It's cold. You could pull a muscle if you run out there without being loose and warm."

"Okay Matilda we will." Skylar responded.

Skylar tore off her jacket and began to stretch and move. She hopped on her feet until she felt some warmth. Then she did a few cartwheels, a flip and a split. She noticed Cory on the sidelines looking at her and she wanted to show him what she could do. Jade, on the other hand, stretched mostly her upper body, moving her arms side to side. Her jumps looked like she had lead in her feet. Debbie a friendly junior leaned over to Skylar and said.

"What is wrong with Jade? She put us all to shame in the tryouts. If they didn't have the rule about having been a cheerleader before, Jade would have easily made the squad. Now, Jade looks like she has cramps in her legs."

"Debbie I'd love to tell you but Jade would be mad at me if I did. Let's put it this way, Jade isn't going to do any routines that cause her skirt to move." Skylar laughed.

Before Debbie could say more, the whistle blew and the players ran on the field. Jade and Skylar moved off the sideline onto the bleachers, putting their heavy coats over their shivering bodies. Debbie smiled at Skylar and then turned her attention toward her first cheerleading assignment.

Jade and Skylar fumed in the first row of the bleachers. Every time Rufus ran for a large gain as the star halfback, Peggy did one of her best routines. At first he pretended not to notice but after a time Rufus started holding the ball out after a big gain so Peggy could see it. Carly focused her routines on Peter, who played end. Peter after watching Rufus also started to hold the ball out toward Carly after he caught a pass. Carly responded by doing her best routine. Skylar made eye contact with Cory the quarterback during warm up but since then the active cheerleaders worked on obtaining his attention. In particular, a senior named Susan focused on Cory. The same thing happened to Jade. She managed to gain Thad's attention during warm up despite her limitations but since then Rita, a junior cheerleader, worked her magic on him. Thad stared as the school's middle linebacker. Jade couldn't resist making comments to Skylar.

"Don't let me run into Rita at school. I took Karate and Judo. I'll slam her to the floor and then punch her lights out."

"I feel the same way. I took a little Tae Kwan Do. I'll punch Susan in the mouth if I see her." Skylar responded.

At just this moment, Ann, a sophomore cheerleader, twisted her ankle on a back flip. She hobbled over to the first row of the bleachers and sat down crying. Matilda yelled at Jade.

"Ann's out. You're up."

Before Jade could stand, Skylar grabbed her hand and said this.

"No remember I have this." Continuing, Skylar said to Matilda.

"Jade's having some leg cramps. I'll substitute."

"Okay hurry up. I think the girls are ready for their next routine." Matilda said.

Jade all alone now started to cry a little. So far her plan worked against her. She certainly hadn't made any progress with Thad. Half time would be in a few minutes. She would have her chance then. She wiped her face and tried to concentrate on what she planned to do.

Thad left the field in a bad mood. He played very poorly in the first half. His linebacker play accounted for much of their successful 10 and 1 season. He made as many as twenty tackles a half. He made only two the first half of this game. Winston had a huge offensive lineman, Big Bob, who made Thad feel like a dwarf. Big Bob made it a point to knock Thad down on every offensive play in the first half. So instead of Thad concentrating on the play in front of him, Thad had to spend his time trying to avoid Big Bob. As a result, Winston had run right through Briar Manor's defenses. Winston already led by three touchdowns. In addition to being ashamed of his play, Thad could barely walk after the pounding he suffered at Big Bob's hands. Mud covered almost all of his body. Seeing Jade only at the beginning of the game, Thad felt grateful she hadn't witnessed his humiliation as a cheerleader. As a freshman, she must be an alternate. As Thad left the field, he suddenly saw Jade motioning to him on the side of the bleachers toward the back. He painfully walked over to her. She grabbed his hand and led him behind the bleachers.

"Thad I have a surprise. I created a special cheerleading routine just for you. I don't want anyone else to see it."

With that statement, Jade performed an outstanding set of flips, splits, jumps and marches while humming a tune. Several times, Jade's underwear flashed in front of Thad. Thad just stared at the spectacle in front of him. He didn't know what to say. When she finished Jade asked.

"Did you like it? I'm still learning some of the moves but it went better than I expected. I think all the dancing I did as a kid helped."

Stumbling a little, Thad finally managed to say.

"I loved it! Jade you have to be the most beautiful and sexy girl alive. If the other guys knew what I just witnessed they would be very jealous. Best of all, I really needed a boost. I didn't play well in the first half. I felt really down and discouraged. Now I'm going to go out there with a new attitude. With you watching me, I know I'll play better."

"Does that mean you're still my boyfriend?" Jade asked.

"Of course, if you still want me to be. After that disastrous Halloween meeting, we thought all of you were mad at us. We came on much too strong. The four of you are just so beautiful it's hard for us to go slowly. Also, all our friends at school kept pressuring us on how far we went with you like it was some baseball game. We felt we had to do something so we could get our friends off our back. Worse still, we ran away like frightened boys when you girls pulled that ghost trick. That was a trick wasn't it?"

"Yeah it was a trick. We'll show you sometime. As to coming on too strong, yeah we felt you did, but you backed away without frightening us too much. Part of the problem is that we just turned fourteen. It's going to take some time for us to work our way into a serious relationship. Anyway we aren't some baseball contest to win. Girls who play those games often get hurt." Jade said.

"That's great news. Our friends have been asking us whether the four of you are available or not. We didn't know what to say. Now we can say no. As to the baseball stuff, we'll just tell our friends it's our business not theirs. Kissing beautiful girls like you is good enough for us. Any way, I have to get back to the locker room. The coach will wonder where I am. He won't be happy after the first half."

Jade reached up and kissed Thad.

"Thad you're finally saying all the right things. Your princess has faith in you. I know you, my knight will do better in the next half." Jade said smiling.

"For you Jade I will or they will have to carry me off on a stretcher."

Jade waved to Thad as he disappeared. She couldn't wait to tell the other girls what she just found out from Thad. They had more influence on these boys than they thought.

The second half of the game went better than the first. After Jade told the rest of the Fab Four what Thad said, they all felt better and happier. Halfway through the second half, another cheerleader hurt her ankle and had to come out. Matilda nodded at Jade and she threw off her coat to join the rest of the squad. Skylar whispered to Jade as she lined up.

"What are you going to do?"

"Give it my best. I want Thad to see me cheering him on."

"What about your underwear?"

"I just changed into my normal underwear. I stuffed the silk underwear in my purse. That underwear served its purpose. Thad and I are back together." Jade answered.

"Jade you sure make life interesting." Skylar laughed.

"Of course I do. I'm a member of the Fab Four."

The Fab Four cheered the Briar Manor team as best they could, but in the end Briar Manor lost by a touchdown. Thad played much better in the second half. He found a way to avoid Big Bob and made the tackles everyone expected him to make. Cory, Peter, and Rufus also played better but they and their teammates couldn't make up the three-touchdown deficit they had at the half. Still, all in all they played well against the best team in the conference and last year's private school champions.

Crying Girl

The next day on their way to Algebra class, the only class they all shared together, the Fab Four saw an overweight girl kneeling and crying in a dark corridor off the main hallway where they walked. Peggy immediately responded.

"I think that's Betty. She's in our Algebra Class. I wonder what could possibly be wrong with her."

"The only thing that makes me cry is boys. Maybe it's that." Jade said.

"No I don't think so. Betty isn't dating at least as far as I know. Maybe we should try to help. Girls need to help each other out. When we cry in public like that it's usually pretty serious." Carly said.

"I agree. I'll ask her what's wrong." Skylar said as she and the rest of the girls approached Betty. Skylar continued.

"Hey Betty what's the matter? You look like your having a tough time today." Skylar said.

Betty looked up with red eyes and her eyes lighted with wonder. She slowly responded.

"I didn't think anyone would see me back here. I have days like today when I just can't show anyone my ugly fat body. It's too embarrassing."

"I know what you mean. I have one of those so-called voluptuous bodies, but believe me my kind of body quickly turns to a fat body when I eat sweets. I love deserts and candy but I just refuse to eat them. That's the only way I can keep my figure. Several times in grade school

I put on too much weight. If I did, I just left the lunch or dinner table when the desserts were served. I also closed my eyes when I walked past a bowl of candy. I even gave away my Halloween candy after hitting every house in my neighborhood last year." Carly said.

"I'm like Carly and do I ever like baked stuff. My mom used to call me the cookie monster even though she constantly tempted me with her home baked pies, cookies, and cakes. As a result, kids used to call me butterball. When I got a little older, I naturally started to lose weight. Also, I began to exercise a lot in sports and just on my own, which helped too. It's a constant battle for me to keep my weight down. I have to bite my lip sometimes when I see big fat oatmeal cookies staring at me." Peggy said.

"I guess I'm the lucky one. I eat like a horse, almost everything in front of me. I'll polish off two or three deserts at a sitting. Despite all this eating, I don't gain an ounce. I just have a very high metabolism or so my doctor says. I burn up everything I eat. Even so I feel guilty when I eat the things other girls don't dare to eat." Jade said.

"I guess that leaves me. I just don't have much of an appetite. I eat half of the food put in front of me. I'm not really sure why that is but I only eat what my body needs. Unlike Jade, I'd get fat if I ate too much but I just don't." Skylar said.

"I can't believe you're sharing all this with me. You're the most beautiful, brilliant and popular girls in the class if not the whole school. I'm at the bottom of the social order; you're at the top." Betty said.

"Even though we call ourselves the Fab Four, we don't think we're better than anyone else at least I don't. We just do the best we can and hope that things go well for us." Carly said.

"Sister you have that right. My relatives were slaves then sharecroppers, which wasn't much better than being a slave. My dad is the first one in our family to make a lot of money. Every time I start feeling better than anyone else, I think back to the way my long ago relatives must have felt. My mom always says you can be anything you want to be or do anything you want to do with the talent god gave you. The only thing that will hold you back is thinking you can't. So, Betty, if your weight is bothering you, you can do something about it. Carly and I decided to do something about it. You can too." Peggy said.

"But it's so hard. There has never been a sweet I didn't like or want to eat. I even dream about food. I sometimes wish I could sew my mouth shut. Anyway, even if I lose weight, I won't be as beautiful or as popular as you." Betty said.

"You're smart enough, that's for sure. Next to Carly and Skylar you're the best student in our Algebra class. Anyway, don't worry about other people and what they can or can't do. You should just be the best you can be. At least, that's what my dad always says." Jade added.

"I'll try to lose weight but I don't know how successful I'll be. I've tried before and failed. Anyway, you girls made me feel better. It's enough that the most popular girls in the class stopped to talk to me when I was feeling bad." Betty said wiping her eyes and standing back on her feet.

"Look Betty, we'll make you a deal. If you lose thirty pounds, you can join the Fab Four, which of course will become the Fab Five." Skylar said.

"Do you really mean it?" Betty said.

"Yeah I do and the rest of us I can tell do too. If you lose thirty pounds, you'll have earned your way into our group." Skylar said.

"I'm going to do it. I'll lose those thirty pounds." Betty said.

"We hope you do." Peggy said.

The rest of the girls in algebra class acted surprised when Betty entered the classroom with the super cool Fab Four on both sides of her. You just never knew what those girls would do next.

Christmas Break

The Fab Four busily prepared for the traditional Christmas Concert, which always occurred just before Christmas and New Year vacation. Skylar spoke.

"Jade and Peggy, you're are going to sound great in the chorus. We'll be cheering for you."

"Yeah, I listened to you the other day at rehearsal. Both of your short solos sounded terrific." Carly added.

"Thanks but we're just doing our part to be part of the Fab Four or Five. Skylar you and Carly are such brains, we need to be special too." Jade said.

"You're our friends. That's special enough. Anyway your grades are pretty good too. Top twenty is better than most of the girls around here. By the way, Skylar, have you made any progress on our plan to see our boyfriends." Carly said.

"A little—On Friday our last day before vacation, I can walk home but everyone else is being picked up by their parents except for Rufus who is riding in a cab to the airport to catch a flight home. Peter is the first to be picked up at 2pm. That basically gives us Friday morning to spend time with each other. Because everyone is leaving, security at both schools will be pretty lax. We should be able to meet our boyfriends at the shopping center and do something from there. I'm asking the boys to meet us at nine am when the shopping center opens. How does that sound?"

"What time should we finish?" Carly asked.

"I asked the boys to be packed and ready to leave the school before they meet us. In this way, we can get them back at a little past one and they can still make their flights or meet their parents."

"What are we gong to do with these guys for four hours?" Peggy asked.

"We shouldn't over plan. We can just hang out at the mall and go for a walk if it's a nice day. We can have lunch too." Jade said.

"I like that idea. If these boys are really going to be our boyfriends, we have to be comfortable with each other even if we don't have anything to do." Carly said.

"Yeah, I agree. Skylar, what have the boys said to your plan?"

"They're fine with it, but I can't say I'm fine with them. It annoys me a little that they don't have any ideas of their own. I thought boys were supposed to romance girls. They should be arranging all this." Skylar said with her lips tightly drawn.

"Welcome to 2014. Constance told me her boyfriend brought her flowers, wrote her love poems, and actually sat outside her window and sang to her." Carly said.

"No, you have to be kidding me. There are a lot of things I wouldn't have liked about her time, but I would 've loved the romance part." Peggy said.

"Yeah, because I sing, I dream about a handsome boy serenading me just like that boy did with Constance." Jade added.

"Briar Manor ought to have a course on how to romance girls and our boyfriends should be the first ones to enroll. Peter, Rufus, Cory, and Thad look good and are good athletes but they are definitely missing this part of their training." Skylar added.

"You can say that again." Carly laughed.

Four days later, the Fab Four paced back and forth in front of the shopping mall. The mall already stood open and the clock just inside showed it to be 9:15. Carly spoke first, irritation working into her voice.

"Correct me if I'm wrong, but this is the second time our so called boyfriends have been late. Not only do they lack romantic skills but they aren't even courteous. I have about ten more minutes in me and then I'm out of here."

"I'm with you Carly. Ever since you mentioned how Constance's boyfriend treated her, I've been thinking about how Thad treats me.

I went out of my way to show him a special cheer with black silk underwear and all I get in response is this." Jade said stomping her feet.

"They have nine minutes left." Skylar added.

"If they use up the full nine minutes, I'll have a hard time controlling my temper." Peggy added.

They did. The boys arrived just as the Fab Four started to leave. The girls didn't move to greet the boys. They just stared at them. Cory raised his hand and spoke.

"We're sorry about being late. Rufus lost his favorite basketball shoes, Nike's no less. He didn't want to leave for vacation without them. We finally found them in the lost and found."

"Yeah, a nice excuse but did you think about calling or texting us with something simple like we're going to be late. We had to do all the work to arrange this, the least you can do is to show up on time or tell us why you can't." Peggy snapped.

A full minute passed before anyone spoke. Finally, Thad managed to say something.

"Okay we messed up on the time but we're still here. Do you want to hang with us or not?"

"We do but it may take some time for our irritation to wear off. Part of the problem we have is attending same sex schools. We can't see each other all the time like in a regular high school. So when we do get together our expectations are high. We want it to feel and be right." Carly said.

"Truce then?" Peter said.

"Yeah, I think we can call one. Why don't we head to the forest preserve beyond the mall. They have nice trails. The snow shouldn't be too deep to walk. I think walking there will improve our mood. It certainly will mine." Jade said.

The four couples walked and talked for almost an hour before the girls finally moved close to their boyfriends. They talked about their schools, their traditions, sports and Peggy's and Jade's singing. They covered a great deal of ground. More time slipped by. When they all sat in a tight circle in a clearing, trying to ward off the cold of early winter, Cory surprised the girls with the question he asked.

"What do you girls know about the Magic Keys of Tanglewood? I've been hearing this story since I was a little kid. Skylar's family is right in the middle of it. We talk about it a lot at Briar Manor. One of our students actually disappeared in the story."

"What should we tell them?" Skylar said.

"That depends how open minded you guys are. We have a way to get closer to the keys than anyone in a very long time." Jade said slowly.

"How?" Rufus asked.

"It has to do a little with Halloween night. Carly why don't you tell them." Peggy added.

"If it is okay with Skylar I will." Carly answered.

"Okay I guess we can trust them even if they like to be late." Skylar said with a little humor in her voice. Carly drew in a deep breath, looked at Peter and began.

"Skylar's house is haunted by a very nice ghost named Constance. She died in 1850 at about our age. She can hear what people in the real world say but most of the time she can only speak to sensitives, people with psychic gifts. Also, ghosts like Constance can only appear in rare circumstances. The problem is that talking to non-sensitives and appearing takes a lot of energy. If a ghost expends too much energy his or her spirit goes to the other world through a bright light. Almost everyone who dies goes into this light and disappears from this world. Constance is the exception.

"Although Skylar's family long suspected a ghost haunted their house, Skylar never had any contact with Constance until I spoke with Constance at the beginning of the school year. As it turns out, I'm a sensitive. For reasons we do not know, Halloween night provides a great deal of extra energy a ghost can absorb. Because of this, Constance told me she might be able to appear or speak to you guys that night and play some tricks that would really scare you. We told her to stand by in case we needed her but we weren't sure whether we wanted to scare you or not. What we did not know is that Constance could absorb even more energy from underneath the school. She and we suspect that this is from the magic keys hidden somewhere down there. Anyway, when you guys came on a little strong, I asked Constance to scare you. For the first time in her spirit history, she both appeared and spoke.

"Constance attended Tanglewood before she became sick and died. She knows a lot about the magic keys and has promised to help us find them. So far, we haven't asked her to do so, but the four of us intend to look for the keys before the end of the school year."

"You told me that the girl in hoop skirt that appeared before us was some kind of trick." A shocked Thad said looking at Jade.

"Thad I didn't think you would accept the truth. Frankly, I have a hard time believing Constance is real sometimes but she is." Jade answered.

"Is she here right now?" Peter asked.

"I can only sense and talk to Constance when she wants me to. She sat right next to Skylar and I and we didn't even know she was there. So all I can say is that as far as I know she isn't here." Carly responded.

"The truth is I never believed that the girl we saw was a fake. She looked very real to me, particularly when she spoke." Rufus said.

"The same goes for me." Peter added.

"Me too." Cory agreed.

An awkward moment passed, then Rufus asked.

"So when you go looking for the keys, do you want us to go along?"

"I don't know about the rest of us, but I sure do." Peggy said.

"I think we all do, but it may not be easy for us to sneak you into the tunnels underneath Tanglewood where we believe the keys are kept." Skylar said.

"Let us worry about sneaking into Tanglewood when you develop your plan. We'll have to rely on you to get us into the tunnels from there. Ever since I was a little boy, I have wanted to go on a real adventure. This certainly qualifies. We could make history for both schools." Cory said.

"Yeah it sounds great." Peter said.

"Even though it is a little scary, I am in too." Thad added.

"Okay we're all agreed. Of course, I'll have to talk to Constance but I can't see why she would object. Oh Constance, you're here after all. That is pretty sneaky of you. I never knew you were here. Constance says she approves of you guys coming along. Oh and she says you guys are really cute and the next time she appears before you she will have something a little more sexy on than a hoop skirt." Carly said.

"I didn't know ghosts still thought about things like that." Peter said laughing.

"Constance is still a girl Peter, ghost or not." Carly replied.

Hidden Diary

After returning to school in January, the Fab Four kept in constant contact with their boyfriends. The search for the keys became one of the favorite topics of their constant e-mails and texts. While their respective schools kept the eight of them very busy, the Fab Four felt increasing pressure to search for the keys. Jade as they huddled in Skylar's dorm room, complained.

"Thad is becoming obsessed with this search for the keys. It really has fired his imagination. I've always been a little nervous about sticking my nose into witchcraft, but I can't put off Thad any longer."

"Cory is worse. He keeps asking the exact date and time we're going. We have to do something. Carly can you ask Constance what she knows? If we are going to make a plan we have to start with her." Skylar added.

"Sure she is right here. Constance is speaking to me now. Here goes.

"About ten years before I attended Tanglewood, a girl named Debbie became obsessed with finding the lost keys. In my day, almost every girl kept a diary and Debbie's diary contained hundreds of pages of detailed notes on the subject, including the witchcraft one had to use to obtain the keys. In her senior year at the school, Debbie's parents died in a horse carriage accident and she hurriedly left the school before graduating never to return. As has happened many times at the school, she left her diary behind. The school placed the diary in its extensive lost and found. Debbie never returned to reclaim it.

"I like several girls before me, looked at the diary but the eagle eyed woman who oversaw the lost and found and the library made sure we put the book back. One day, I decided to hide the book. I found a loose brick behind a small cabinet in the wall and placed the diary behind the brick. After I did that, the librarian furious that the diary had been lost or stolen would not allow any girl into the lost and found unless she watched them. I never saw the diary again. For all I know, the diary is still behind the brick. I never told anyone where I hid it. The lost and found is kept locked. Only relatives or the actual owners of materials are allowed in the lost and found to retrieve them. "

"Do you remember anything about what the book said?" Jade asked.

Constance speaking though Carly said.

"Debbie never believed that the keys could be accessed in the regular tunnels underneath the school. She claimed to have explored every inch of them and found nothing. Rather she believed the keys could be found in a secret tunnel. According to Debbie, this tunnel could be reached from a hidden entrance at the edge of the school's tunnels or from an outside entrance deep in the woods. Debbie also suspected the hidden tunnel might be the same as the tunnel connecting our house to the school. Reportedly after the duke built the school and problems began to develop between the colonies and England, he constructed a tunnel to connect his house to the school, which at that time was his sister Prudence's house, in case American rebels invaded either his house or the school. The duke at first claimed to be a loyal citizen of the crown but very late in the American Revolution he switched his allegiance to the American rebels. Unfortunately, this is all I read of the diary. I know it contained much more information but I just didn't have the time to read most of it. By the way, I've looked many times for the entrance to the duke's tunnel to the school but never found a trace of it."

"Cousin that's really neat. Obviously, we have to find Debbie's diary if we can. I think the room Constance speaks of is now the archive. Lost and found items are now kept in a large locked closest in the headmistress' office. Girl reporters sometimes go in the archives to find background for articles they are writing about the school. Like many Worthington's before me I've already joined the Tanglewood Times as a reporter. I've been thinking about doing an article on the origins of woman's athletic teams at the school. As part of my research, I'm pretty sure the school would allow me access to the archive room. I could check the brick hiding place and see if the diary is still there." Skylar said with some excitement.

"Cool," Peggy said.

"Maybe I can search the archive room before you go in there. I can see if the diary is still there and if it is, tell you where its hiding place is. Ghosts like me can see in the dark but only in general shapes. It would help a lot for someone to put some light inside the room. If I remember correctly, the room has no windows." Constance said through Carly.

"Okay just before bed, all of us will go down to the archives. With a little luck, the switch to turn on the light in the archives will be outside the door. If it is, Constance will search for the diary and then come back outside to tell us what she finds. If not, Constance will follow me into the archive tomorrow when I do my research. Carly will wait outside the archive room. When and if Constance locates the diary, she will tell Carly where it is and she will in turn tell me." Skylar said working out the details as she talked.

"Sounds like a plan to me." Peggy said. The others just nodded in agreement. Several hours later the girls and Constance gathered by the archive door, which lay at the end of a corridor in the main basement. Jade served as a lookout in case anyone came to the little used corridor. As luck would have it, a switch appeared just outside the archive door. When Carly hit the switch a dim light shone under the door. Constance through Carly said.

"Okay I'm going inside. If its too scary in there I'm coming right back out here. "

The Fab Four paced outside waiting for Constance to return. Jade continued to watch for unwanted guests. Finally after ten minutes, Carly spoke as Constance.

"I'm back. It's really dusty in there, but, as a ghost the dust doesn't bother me. I found the loose brick but I can't tell if the diary is still behind it. One good thing—there is no longer a small cabinet in front of the brick. To find it cousin, you walk to the end of the shelves on your right, turn right and walk directly to the brick wall. The brick is located at your shoulder height close to the intersecting back wall. If you push on all the bricks there, you'll find the one that is loose."

"Good-I'll try to get into the archive room tomorrow. The Worthington name still counts for something around here, so I'm feeling good about my chances." Skylar said.

Jade who rejoined her friends said. "Wow this is great but let's get out of here. I don't want to explain to anyone why we're here?

"Neither do I. Let's go." Peggy said as she began to march back down the hall.

As predicted, Skylar didn't have a very hard time gaining permission to visit the archive. Skylar told the headmistress she searched for a certain Cindy's diary, who played field hockey for Tanglewood in 1912. Skylar would look for this diary but of course from the moment she stepped into the archives Skylar searched for Barbara's lost diary. Skylar found the loose brick with little trouble but unfortunately the diary no longer hid behind it. In desperation, she searched the wall for another loose brick on the off chance that someone else found the diary but returned it to a different place in the archive. At first, Skylar saw nothing then a brick near the floor caught her eye. The mortar around the brick looked very worn and crumbled much more so than the mortar around the rest of the bricks. Kneeling, Skylar removed the brick with little trouble. To her great surprise, Skylar found an old diary behind the brick. She rapidly identified the diary as Barbara's but after scanning through it found some writing on the last several pages in someone else's hand. She read the passage with growing excitement.

"Debbie had been right all those many years ago. She identified the southeast corner of the tunnel network as the likely place for the duke's tunnel. As her diary instructed I pounded the wall with a hammer on both sides of the corner looking for a hollow sound. At first like Debbie, I had no success. I couldn't tell the difference in the sounds the hammer made. Then I pulled out the stethoscope I brought from the biology lab and repeated the hammer strokes up and down the wall on both sides. Ten feet to the right of the corner, I could distinctly hear the difference with the stethoscope. I found the secret tunnel!

"I outlined the hidden door by doing my hammer striking and when I did so I explored the area where a release would be if the door opened from the left as it should. To my amazement, when I struck the most likely area, the hidden door suddenly swung wide open. I quickly stepped into the tunnel, which probably hadn't been used in over a hundred years. From the moment I did, the world around me started to change. I heard strange unearthly sounds and the air seemed to sizzle with energy. The farther I went down the tunnel the more powerful the energy and the louder the sounds. I became very frightened, but driven by curiosity I kept walking, my lantern lighting the way. After a half hour, a corridor suddenly appeared on my left. There could be little doubt that the loud sounds and now the almost unbearable energy came from this corridor. I felt like my skin burning as it does on a sunny summer day. Against every instinct I have, I walked down this frightening corridor until it ended with an astounding sight: a shimmering transparent wall with a solid oak door behind it. I put my hand on the shimmering wall but the wall proved to be impenetrable. It also felt very hot to the touch, giving me a painful burn on my hand. Debbie said in her diary that to pass into the world where the key lay a spell had to be performed but I hadn't brought the materials I needed to do the spell. So I returned back the way I came and carefully closed the hidden door so it once again became almost impossible to find. I did, however, place a rock in front of it so I could find it again.

"For the next month, I debated the pros and cons of returning to the shimmering wall and performing the ceremony that would bring down the wall. I knew full well that the magic keys were somewhere behind that door. In the end I decided not to return. I sensed death and evil as I stood before that shimmering wall and as a young girl had no wish to end up as a lock on the main gate of Tanglewood. You may judge me to be a coward if you like, but I think I made the right decision. When I had the chance, I returned Debbie's book to the lost and found and placed it behind another brick that I found to be loose. I didn't want relatives of Constance Worthington who I discovered placed the diary there returning and finding Debbie's diary. Indeed I didn't want anyone to ever find this diary again. Some things are better left undisturbed. The Keys of Tanglewood are one of those things. Sandra."

Barley able to contain her excitement, Skylar quickly found the other diary she sought and placed it and Debbie's diary in her book bag. Skylar left the archive key with the headmistress's secretary and ran to find the rest of the Fab Four so they could read the diary.

Serenade

A short time after finding the book, the girls studied as hard as they could. Final exams began the next day. All four of them stared at their computers carefully going over their long class notes. In the very quiet room, which usually echoed with the chatter of the four girls, Jade suddenly leaped out of her seat. Almost yelling, she cried.

"I have to take a break. I'm going to turn into a flat chested nerd with heavy ugly glasses if I study these algebra problems any harder. Let's talk about our boyfriends. A new boy, Chet keeps e-mailing me. We met at the Christmas concert. He sang for Briar Manor. He has a great voice. He says so many sweet things to me. Chet knows how to treat a girl."

"What about Thad. I mean you did a full cheerleading routine for him in your silk underwear. Are you thinking about cheating on him?" Peggy asked glad to stop studying for a while.

"I don't really know. As I've said, a girl needs romance. Chet isn't as muscular or as handsome as Thad, but his voice, oh my god his voice." Jade replied.

"Sometimes Jade I think you're in love with being in love, but you know that isn't necessarily a bad thing. Romance is what keeps us girls going." Carly said, stretching her arms. Carly already knew the history material in front of her.

"I agree. That's why I spend all my spare time reading romance novels. What can be better than that? Of course with these pesky exams, the sexy man in my latest novel hasn't even kissed the heroin yet. I can't wait until vacation when I can find out what happens. Hey wait a minute, did you just hear something hit our window?" Skylar added.

"Yeah, come on ladies quick, there is a boy under our windows and some flowers he threw on our window sill. He has a guitar. He looks a little familiar but I don't really know him. I don't think he is for me, but I sure wish he was." Carly said running to the window.

"Oh my god! It's Chet. Open the window. Wait until you hear his voice." Jade said running to the window to stand next to Carly. Peggy and Skylar quickly squeezed next to their friends.

As soon as Jade stood in the window, Chet smiled and bowed. He called up to the four girls who now all stood in the window.

"Wow four beautiful girls! I think that's really going to make me sing better. But I came for you Jade. I want you to pick your favorite love song. I'll sing it the best I can. You girls need to take a little break from studying for exams."

"Crazy in Love" then, Jade yelled back giggling as she did so.

"Great, I know that one. Here goes."

When Chet launched into the song, his guitar providing perfect accompaniment, the Fab Four swooned. Chet's voice made the average looking boy into a potent sex symbol. Strong powerful football players become one thing, this great singer became something all together different when he sang. Chet displayed amazing talent. When he finished, the girls clapped loudly. Chet bowed and said.

"Thank you ladies. Beauty like yours deserves this kind of serenade, but I've a reason for being here. Every time I can Jade, I'm going to serenade you and bring you flowers until you promise to go out with me. If you break my heart and say no, I'll have to sing for one of your room mates instead." Chet said.

"Chet I don't think I can answer you right now, but I'm not going to say no to you. I can't. Oh darn, I hear someone shouting outside. I think one of the guards is coming, but don't go just yet. I have a present for you." Jade said hurriedly.

Jade ran to her dresser and pulled out her black silk panties. She rushed to the window and threw them at Chet. The rest of the Fab Four just stared in amazement.

Chet picked up the panties and put them in his guitar. He smiled up at Jade, bowed, and said.

"My love, my one true love. I'll keep these always. You'll see me soon. I'll keep singing to you until you say yes."

With that word, Chet ran off toward the woods and disappeared. A guard chased him for a while but Chet planned his escape well. The guard knowing he wouldn't catch the fast Chet stopped at the edge of the woods and shook his head. The girls could hear him laughing a little. The shock of what just happened wore off Peggy first. She turned to Jade and said.

"Are you crazy, throwing your racy panties to that boy? If he brags about the panties at school, Thad will find out the panties are yours. After all he had plenty of time to look at them when you did your cheerleading routine."

"Yeah, if Thad finds out Chet has your panties, he'll kill him. "Carly added.

"You girls are just jealous. I didn't see a boy down there singing to you and bringing you flowers. I had to give Chet something for taking the risk he did, for being romantic. I thought about the black panties and just reacted. I never thought about how Thad might feel about it." Jade answered.

"What I don't understand is why you would do something extreme like throw Chet your panties and not agree to date him. It doesn't make any sense." Skylar said.

"Sure it does. You can't say yes right away. You don't want a boy to think that he has you under his thumb. That is why I said maybe." Jade answered.

"If you can't find any time on your schedule for him, I think I can fit Chet in. Rufus wouldn't know what romance is if it hit him on the head." Peggy said.

"Yeah, the only thing Cory can throw at my window is a football." Skylar added.

"Are there any other romantic Briar Manor boys who can sing like Chet? Maybe I can hook up with one of them." Carly said.

"Sorry girls, there are no other Chets and by the way, keep your hands off. I'm not only going to say yes next time but I'm going to kiss

Chet as hard as I can. Chet isn't getting away, not if I can help it." Jade said.

"You better hurry. I have no problem saying yes to the right guy the first time." Peggy said teasing Jade.

"I will, then life will be perfect. I'll have a boy for my every mood." Jade said.

"I can't keep more than one boy going at a time. I have enough trouble with Cory who thinks he has full access to all the females his age just because he can throw a football." Skylar said.

"Peter thinks the same thing, just because he can catch one. Oh and one more thing. Constance is here. She is getting really sneaky. She says Chet is definitely her type and belongs more in her time than in ours." Carly added.

"Sorry Constance, Chet is in our time." Jade replied.

Peggy shook her head as the girls moved back from the window and reluctantly walked toward their desks and waiting study papers. Before she sat down Peggy turned and addressed Jade. "No matter what you might think Jade, having two boyfriends is going to be trouble. I just know it."

Tunnels of Tanglewood

The Fab Four tingled with excitement. After returning to school following winter break, they carefully planned their trip into the tunnels underneath Tanglewood. Each read Debbie's diary at least those parts dealing with the magic keys in detail over the holiday. They carefully copied the pages so they could do so. The Fab Four felt very confident. They excelled in the first semester. As usual, Skylar received straight A's making her number one in the class while Carly received one A minus and the rest A's making her number two in the class. Jade and Peggy also did well as top twenty students.

The Fab Four collected the necessary equipment and ingredients to light their way into the tunnels, find the hidden door and perform the spell that would open the shimmering wall. Constance, on the other hand, expressed lingering doubts about the quest. She worried that they would be dealing with forces they didn't understand or know how to control. Nonetheless, Constance pledged to go with her new friends whatever her reservations.

The girls gathered in Skylar's room after the hall monitor checked that they hadn't left their rooms. Peggy spoke first.

"We have to get moving. Sometimes the hall monitor will make one last check. Has everyone stuffed their beds so it looks like we're sleeping? The fact that we appeared asleep when she came by this time doesn't mean she won't check again."

"Don't worry, all the beds are stuffed as well as they can be stuffed with pillows and blankets. Jade do you have everything in the back pack?" Skylar asked.

"Yes, but if it gets too heavy someone else will have to carry it." Peggy responded.

"That won't be a problem. I asked our boyfriends to come. Thad and Cory will meet me by the back door in fifteen minutes. I'll lead them to the basement. Rufus and Peter couldn't come because of basketball tryouts. Thad can carry the backpack. He is certainly strong enough." Jade said.

"Jade, I know we talked about our boyfriends coming, but we never really made a decision about whether to ask them or not." Skylar said.

"That's true but we face some serious dangers. Having big strong football players with us can help." Jade answered.

"Okay there isn't anything we can do about it now. We may need some boy strength somewhere down the line, but sneaking boys down to the basement carries some additional risks of being caught. Anyway, your inviting the boys tells us a lot about our relationships with our boyfriends. Peggy and I now know that ours can't always be counted on to show up when we face danger." Carly said with a little anger in her voice.

"I agree with you on that one." Peggy added stomping her foot.

"Okay, now that the addition of the two boys including my boyfriend is decided, I officially start this quest by taking the first step out of the door. By the way, as I promised, I took the key to open the gate to the tunnels from the headmistress' office. No one ever uses it and I doubt they will miss it." Skylar said as she marched forward.

As luck would have it, Jade managed to sneak the boys into the basement and the rest of the girls made it into the basement without being seen. The girls almost bumped into a teacher who lived at the school but at the last moment they ducked into a storage closet. The preoccupied teacher didn't even notice them. The boys and Jade heard a janitor's heavy boots rounding a corner, but Jade pulled the boys into the girls' bathroom just before he appeared. Before the boys could say anything, Jade said.

"This is the last time you'll ever see the inside of a girl's bathroom. At least this time of the night, there aren't any girls in here."

The boys just snickered a little and didn't say anything.

The entrance to tunnels lay at the end of a long mostly dark corridor. No one had bothered to replace many of the bulbs that had gone out. The girls had to turn on their battery powered lanterns and flashlights to find their way. The rusty heavy metal door at the end of the corridor had a single large padlock on it. Skylar fitted the key in the lock but the lock resisted being turned. Thad and Cory had to help twist the key before the lock reluctantly opened. With the boys pushing with all their strength, the door creaked open on its rusty hinges. The tunnel stretched into the distance. The girls and boys could see movement and heard squeaks.

"Don't worry those are rats. The tunnels have always had rats living in them. They won't bother you if you don't' bother them. The spiders are a little different. They will bite if they fall on you. No not really, I'm just kidding." Skylar said with more confidence than she felt.

"This is really hard on me. I hate both spiders and rats and everything else that creeps and crawls." Carly complained. At just this moment, a large spider landed on Carly's shoulder. She screamed. Laughing, Peggy brushed the spider off Carly and it scurried away into the darkness. Carly spoke once again after she gained her breath."

"I almost had a heart attack. What if that spider was poisonous? I could die."

Skylar chuckled as she responded.

"Almost all spiders are poisonous. That's how they kill the bugs they eat, but of the thousands of species of spiders only a few have poison strong enough to bother a person. We're just too big."

"Yeah I know that but there are still some dangerous ones. Still, I'm glad I sent one last e-mail to Peter. I figured I might die on this quest and I wanted him to know that I liked him." Carly admitted.

"You didn't. I sent one too." Peggy added.

"Hey, Skylar and Jade you didn't send one to us did you?" Cory said with a smile on his face.

"Well I did send one to you Cory. I didn't know you were coming until Jade told me." Skylar admitted.

"Hey I'm the one left out here. I doubt you sent me one Jade as you invited us to come. Anyway, I should be mad at you Jade. You gave your sexy underwear to Chet. I could deck that pipsqueak with one punch. And I almost did until my friends talked me out of it. They said I would be thrown out of the school and it would wreck our football team if I left. I couldn't do that to my football buddies. Still every time I see Chet, I ball up my fist and have to look away before I punch him. What were you thinking? I hope you didn't kiss him. If you did, I will really be mad. Then I won't care if they throw me out. I'll put the guy in the hospital." Thad said.

"No Thad I didn't kiss him and didn't agree to go out with him. Still, he was very romantic. He sang for me. That is why I gave him my underwear. Oh and you're right. I didn't send you an e-mail because I knew you were coming with us. " Jade admitted.

"Jade what am I going to do with you?" Thad complained.

"Just be patient and love me, that's all any girl wants." Jade replied.

"Okay can we worry about this relationship thing later? We're on a quest that could be very dangerous. Let's focus on that." Carly complained.

"Alright I'll stop talking about the underwear thing for the rest of this quest, but Jade we need to come to an understanding on this issue. You are either my girlfriend or you aren't." Thad said.

"Okay Thad but think about who I invited to go on this quest with me. It wasn't Chet. I don't think the witches are going to care very much about the way Chet sings." Jade said.

After that statement, the six of them fell quiet, looking staring anxiously at the old tunnel walls. Then, a half-hour later with compass in hand Skylar made an announcement.

"According to my compass this is the southeast corner. Let's look for Sandra's rock. "

The girls and two boys looked high and low for the rock but didn't find anything near where the door supposedly stood. After more than a hundred years, the girls and boys would have been surprised if they found the rock where Sandra said it would be. Finally, Skylar spoke.

"Constance if you are here could you find the door?"

Speaking for Constance Carly spoke," Yes if its there I'll find it. I can go through walls but it's a little uncomfortable for me. Being inside a wall feels a little like being smothered. Point to where you think the door is most likely to be and I will go through the wall."

"I don't know about you Thad but it really freaks me out that Carly talks to that ghost." Cory said.

"Yeah it does, but that's what makes these girls so interesting. Some of the other girls we talk to are pretty boring by comparison." Thad responded.

"And what girls are those?" Jade snapped.

"You're not the only one that can play the field. Remember the four of us are football stars. We have plenty of girls approaching us." Thad said with a little smile.

"Come on you guys, you promised to bury this relationship thing while we're down here." Carly said.

"Okay, truce but Thad hasn't heard the last of this if he has been two timing me." Jade huffed.

The Fab Four and the two boys, once again focusing on the quest deliberated at length and pointed to a spot to the right of the southeast corner. Constance gathering all her courage moved through the wall in the exact spot they pointed. Several minutes passed. The Fab Four and the two boys waited anxiously for Constance to return. They paced back and forth in front of the wall next to the corner. They looked anxiously at Carly but she remained silent. Finally Carly spoke on Constance's behalf.

"The door is five feet to the right of where you pointed. I'm going to have Carly point to the place where the release lever should be. I can tell you the energy in the hidden tunnel is very powerful."

Carly pointed to the place where Constance believed the hidden lever lay. All the quest team felt the area until Peggy finally raised her hand.

"I found it but the lever is old and rusty. Thad I need your strength to move it. If that is okay Jade."

"It's alright but don't get too close to Peggy Thad."

Peggy and Thad pulled the lever with all their strength. Finally, the lever rotated backward and the door moved revealing the hidden tunnel behind it. The quest group moved cautiously into the old tunnel and headed for what they hoped would be the location of the keys. As Sandra had all those years ago, the Fab Four and the two boys felt the powerful sizzling energy and heard the strange sounds. After walking in this strange world for a while, an odd thing happened. Constance began to materialize before everyone's eyes. At first, she appeared transparent but as they drew closer to the source of the energy surrounding them her form became more solid. For the first time, Constance spoke for herself.

"I can't believe it. This can't be happening. I have a form. I can talk. I don't think I'm alive as you girls and boys are but I'm more than the ghost I have been for so long."

"Welcome cousin! You're or were a beautiful girl. I looked up your picture, but that black and white picture in the family archives doesn't do you any justice." Skylar said with wonder.

"Yeah, too bad you're only a ghost. I can see spending some time with you." Cory said.

"If you do that, I can see kicking you with some very real shoes." Skylar said her blue eyes flashing.

"I'm beginning to think that having you guys along is a mistake. Let's focus on the quest again. Please." Carly said.

The Fab Four and the two boys slowly nodded in agreement. Constance now spoke to all of them.

"Thanks to all of you for the compliments. At least I'm appearing as a healthy fourteen year old rather than the sick one that died of that terrible disease. I'm happy to be here with all of you but I can sense evil. I'm worried about you my new friends. I'm already dead and can just go into the light if the evil becomes too threatening. You on the other hand may have to deal with some very real physical threats." Constance said.

"Thanks for you concern, Constance, but we're committed to this adventure. At least we want to take the adventure farther than Sandra did. This magic key mystery has gone on far too long. It needs to be solved once and for all." Peggy said.

"Yeah I agree. This is our mission as the Fab Four or rather five now that you are here Constance. I guess you guys are also included." Jade added.

"Ladies and gentlemen I don't know if you have noticed but that's the corridor leading to the shimmering wall and door." Carly said pointing to the corridor coming up on their left.

The Fab Five and the two boys now starred at the scary corridor. As described in Sandra's account strange loud noises came from the corridor and the air seemed to be on fire with energy. The diary did not mention, however, the terrible stench coming from the corridor. It smelled like a sewer.

Skylar wrinkling her nose made the first comment.

"Wow does that smell awful. Did the school sewer back up here?"

"I don't know. If this smell gets any stronger I think I'll be sick. Can it be coming from the other world lying behind the oak door?" Jade said.

"There is only one way to find out. We walk up to the shimmering wall if of course there is such a wall." Peggy commented.

The girls and boys holding their noses marched down the corridor. As the diary described a powerful transparent shimmering wall with a large oak door behind it confronted the girls. The smell didn't become any worse but at the same time didn't become any better.

"This is it ladies and of course gentlemen. Unload the magic supplies. We aren't going any further if we can't lower that shimmering wall." Jade announced.

"Move away. We don't need those supplies. No barrier is going to stop me." Thad said as he approached the shimmering wall with his linebacker swagger. While everyone protested, Thad put his hand on the wall; then leaped back almost two feet yelling "owe".

"Are you all right? Don't scare me like that." Jade cried.

Thad slowly regained his feet and sheepishly said.

"Yeah it kind of felt like that giant tackle pushing me down but I feel okay if a little dazed. I guess we'll need those magic supplies after all."

The rest of the group nodded and pulled all the ingredients out of Skylar's witchcraft game. This time when they lit the candles the affect against the shimmering wall mesmerized the girls and boys. As the girls set up the pentagram and the boys helped, Constance spoke.

"I saw you girls do this at the house. I can already feel the energy coming out of the center of the pentagram like last time. It's making me stronger." Constance commented.

When the girls completed their preparations, Carly turned toward Skylar and asked.

"What do we do now? The magic spell that came with the game evokes spirits. We need to take down a barrier."

"I have that covered. First I say the basic evocation spell again as follows: Hic en Spiritum; Sed Non Incorpore, Evokare Lemures de Mortius; Decretum Espugnare; De Angelus Balberith; En Inferno

Inremeablis. "This evokes the power of the spirit. Then I will use the more specific spell for dissolving the barrier: Se Dissolvant Claustrum Falsa. As before we must each say the last phrase five times. That includes you guys too." Skylar replied.

"Hey we don't know anything about this spell thing, so we are just going along for the ride. But I have to say this is pretty neat if a little scary. We'll just copy what you do." Cory said.

"I sure hope this works. Last time we had water glasses and we had to do the spell at sunset. It's past sunset now." Peggy said.

"I think it'll be alright. We do have the soil and the salt and put a small amount of water from our plastic water bottles into some small glasses. Also, we're saying the right words." Carly answered.

The girls and boys waited for Skylar to walk to the center of the pentagram and say the spirit spell. When she finished, they all carefully said the door dissolve spell. At first, nothing happened. Then, the shimmering wall began to glow brighter and brighter until it dissolved in a blinding flash.

"Wow that was neat!" Thad said.

"Yeah you girls really know how to show your men a good time." Cory agreed.

With the girls giggling a little, the Fab Five and the two boys wasted no time in walking the three short steps to the oak door. Skylar grabbed the door and addressed her friends.

"Are you ready?"

"Yes," they all responded.

With surprising ease, Skylar opened the door. What lay beyond startled the girls and boys: trees, old looking small houses and meadows spreading out before them into the distance. A well-worn path ended at the door. Yet, this landscape didn't look at all like a real world. Instead, everything seemed slightly out of focus, somewhat dark and the vibrant strong colors seemed very wrong. The trees for example looked purple in the strange light. Also, the energy they had all felt clearly came from this strange world as did the foul smells and strange noises. For several minutes, the girls and boys just stared. Suddenly, a face appeared in the strange world, growing larger by the moment. Although an attractive face, a snarl formed at the lips. Carly remembered the face from her dreams. She moved back a step. Soon the face grew to fill almost the entire opening. The lips moved slowly, but the girls and boys couldn't understand the words. The hands of the fearsome face appeared and made a gesture as if pulling something. Constance, who had kept her distance, rapidly moved toward the opening. Skylar reached out for Constance as she floated past her but Constance hands went right through Constance.

"Constance, don't go in there. That has to be Elizabeth. I don't even what to think what that evil witch will do to you."

"Cousin help me, I can't stop!" Constance cried.

As Constance entered the World In Between, Skylar, not thinking ran after her. Carly crying out followed Skylar.

"Skylar you can't go in there. You'll be lost forever."

The other two girls and boys in a state of shock didn't follow their friends right away. The witch frightened them too much. Jade, however, soon changed her mind.

"I'm going into this world and help my friends. Are you coming Peggy, Thad and Cory? You Cory even more than us need to go rescue your girlfriend." Jade said.

"Yeah I guess. You go first." Peggy answered.

"No wait a minute. This is for a boy to do. Stand aside. Here I go." Cory said.

Cory waked toward the opening but couldn't move passed the doorstep. A new invisible wall blocked him. Thad joined him but had no more luck than Cory.

Jade said looking a little annoyed.

"Obviously boys aren't allowed. Move aside. I'll go inside."

Jade moved up next to Thad and promptly put her head into the World In Between but she couldn't take the rest of her body with her. She cried out.

"Help me you guys I'm stuck. Push me inside or pull me out but don't leave me like this."

"I'm having a very hard time hearing you but I think you're saying that you are stuck. Okay I'll try to help but can you see Carly and Skylar?" Peggy said.

"Yes, but not very well. Everything is very fuzzy. I'll yell at them."

"CARLY AND SKYLAR HELP ME, I'M STUCK."

After a few minutes, Jade spoke again.

"They didn't respond. Elizabeth must be blocking my voice and preventing Skylar and Carly from seeing me. They looked right at me as if I wasn't here."

"Alright you can't stay that way. First we will push you. If that doesn't work, we'll pull you instead." Peggy said.

Peggy, Cory and Thad pushed Jade with all their strength but Jade didn't go any further into the World In Between. Peggy spoke again.

"That didn't work, so we're going to pull you instead."

Thad surrounded Jade's waist with his arms and Peggy and Cory grabbed on to Thad and Jade the best they could. Thad cried out.

"Okay on two all of us pull. One and two."

The three of them pulled backward with all their strength. Suddenly, the World In Between released Jade and she fell backward into Thad's arms. All four of them fell on the floor. Jade couldn't resist saying.

"Okay Thad that's enough. You can let go now. I'm free. I'm still mad at you about the other girls you've been talking to."

As the girls and boys regained their feet, they saw a frightening Elizabeth emerge from the very fuzzy looking world in front of them. The witch laughed at the girls and boys then swept her right arm outward. As she did so, the door suddenly closed in the two boys and girls faces. Peggy tried to open the door again cursing as she did so but it wouldn't move. Jade, Thad and Cory also tugged on the door with little effect. The two girls and boys for the first time could faintly hear Carly and Skylar crying out.

"Help us! We don't want to be in here all alone with this terrible witch."

Peggy called back. "We'll find a way to help you. We don't leave our friends behind, but the witch has locked the door. We can't move it."

Unfortunately this time, her statement received no response. Carly, Skylar and Constance seemed to be gone, swallowed up in the strange world behind the door.

Jade broke the silence.

"What are we going to do? Carly, Skylar and Constance are in trouble and we're at fault. God knows what that witch will do to them. As you could see, I tried to get into the World In Between but the witches' world wouldn't let all of me go inside. "

"I don't know how to fight a powerful witch. We should all be in there helping but I just froze when the witch appeared. She had the most frightening eyes I've ever seen. Maybe if I tried to go inside with Skylar and Carly I could have made it all the way in." Peggy said.

"We all froze. I struggle with some of the biggest and toughest lineman you have ever seen and I couldn't move a muscle. As boys, Cory and I should have done something but we didn't. I just couldn't deal with a real live witch." Thad said.

"You can say that again about her eyes. I'll be seeing them in my nightmares. And I don't think you could have entered the World In Between any more than I could. For some reason, Elizabeth doesn't want the rest of us in there." Jade said.

"Yeah, Carly and Skylar relatives go all the way back to the time and place this all happened but as far as I know my relatives don't." Jade said.

"Neither do mine. My distant relatives were slaves in Alabama." Peggy said.

"I'm just a regular guy. My dad is a construction worker. I have no relation to this long ago world." Thad said.

"I do. My relatives go all the way back to when this school started, but I had no more luck than the rest of you. Maybe she doesn't like boys." Cory said.

"Well whatever the reason, we'll find a way to help. I know we will." Jade said.

"Yeah we're part of the Fab Four or Five if you count Constance. Fabs like us always find a way, especially when we have a couple of Briar Manor boys with us." Peggy agreed.

Aftermath

After spending almost a half hour trying to open the door to the World In Between, Peggy, Cory, Thad and Jade reluctantly moved out of the corridor. The shimmering wall re-appeared as soon as they did. Peggy and Jade left the magic materials from the Necromancer kit behind. They expected to use it again when they figured out a way to enter the world that trapped their friends. As the girls and boys walked down the corridor, Cory spoke.

"I don't believe anything I just saw. I can't. But I'm really upset Skylar is in that place and I can't do anything about it. Some knight I turned out to be. Worse still, I don't know what Thad and I can do to help you. We aren't even supposed to be here. We'll be punished if anyone finds out. Still, if you girls really get in trouble, I guess I can confirm your story but that is about all I can do." Cory said looking at his feet.

"Yeah Cory is right. You girls would've been better off on your own, but like Cory I'm willing to stand up and confirm your story, even though I have a hard time believing it myself. It is the least I can do." Thad said.

"Peggy and I have this. We shouldn't have brought you guys into it. All this key stuff is part of Tanglewood history not Briar Manor history except for the boy drawn into it. Any adults we talk to won't believe our story anyway so exposing you guys to punishment doesn't make a lot of sense. Still, I have to say I appreciate you coming today to back us up. You did help us in many ways. That is what boyfriends should be doing." Jade said suddenly kissing Thad on the lips.

Thad smiled and said.

"Am I forgiven?"

"Yeah but don't get any ideas." Jade laughed. Unfortunately, Peggy didn't laugh along with Thad and Jade. She complained.

"Yeah and where is Rufus when I need him? The next time we get together he isn't going to find me to be very affectionate."

As the four of them walked back down the corridor, they fell into silence. After leaving the secret tunnel, the group placed several rocks by the hidden entrance to the secret tunnel and scratched the wall near the hidden lever. When they reached the basement, Jade took the boys to the back entrance to the school while Peggy walked up to her dorm room. Way after hours, they had to hide from both guards and school monitors on the way back. When Jade finally joined Peggy back in their room, Peggy and Jade instead of going to sleep, discussed what they would do next.

"We have big problems. The school officials will after a few hours be questioning us on where Carly and Skylar went. We can say they're sick or went back to their homes but our lies will soon be discovered. When the school authorities find out that Skylar and Carly are truly gone, the police and everyone else will come. How we can tell them or anyone else the truth? They will think we're nuts and belong in a mental hospital. At the same time, we have to lower the shimmering wall again and find a way to open the oak door and somehow push ourselves into that strange world past the invisible wall. Maybe we can do that with magic, but how can we do that with adults watching us." Peggy worried.

"Yeah I've been thinking the same thing. Maybe we can say that Skylar and Carly talked a lot about their boyfriends and sneaked off to be with them. If that doesn't work, we can say that they decided to go home for the weekend. I'm sure Thad and Cory would back us up and after today convince Rufus and Peter to do the same. We can say that we're only guessing because our friends left without telling us where they were going. Until the adults find out that Carly and Skylar didn't go home or to see their boyfriends, we will be off the hook. Of course, when they don't find the girls they'll really pressure us to say more." Jade said in response.

"Yeah that sounds the best. It may give us enough time to try and open the oak door. As we said before, I think the witch planned on having Constance, Skylar and Carly in there but not the rest of us. Remember she hates the Worthington's, so she would want Constance and Skylar. Maybe Carly has a connection to the keys too but if she does, Carly never told anyone what that might be. As to the boys, I guess they just don't fit into the whole key thing."

"I guess not. Anyway, let's get a few hours sleep. I'm too tired to do anything more tonight. We will find a way of getting our friends back, I know we will." Peggy said.

"I sure hope you're right. I for one am going to be thinking about what happened all night. I may not sleep very well." Jade added.

World In Between

Meanwhile, Constance, who remained visible, Skylar and Carly tried very hard to adjust to the weird world in which they found themselves. For some strange reason, Elizabeth disappeared after closing the oak door. They called out to their friends beyond the door but they couldn't make any sense of the faint responses they heard. They thought their friends may have called for them but couldn't hear them very well in this strange place. Alone now, Skylar and Carly tried to open the oak door from their side but couldn't make it move. Elizabeth must have placed some kind of spell on it. Finally, Skylar said.

"Now that we're here and can't go back, we might as well look for the keys. Maybe we're meant to be here."

"I can understand why Elizabeth wanted you and me here Skylar, we are after all Worthington's but why did Elizabeth pull Carly in here?" Constance said.

"I think I have the answer. My family, the Bradshaw's sent girls to this school from its start. Apparently, a distant cousin, Rebecca, spent a lot of time with Samantha, the girl who teased Elizabeth. I imagine Elizabeth sensed that connection in me." Carly responded.

"I never knew you had this connection but it makes sense. Even after more than two hundred years, Elizabeth still wants to get even with her tormentors. Talk about holding a grudge, this woman really does." Skylar said.

"Yes she be the meanest of witches," said another woman who like Elizabeth seemed to have magic power and suddenly appeared in front of the girls. A Calico cat walked at the woman's side.

"Who are you?" Constance asked.

"My name be Rachel. I'm the woman who knowest how to stop Elizabeth but lost meeself in here doing so. This be Calico. He spendeth time with us here."

"Yes my distant relative the duke hired you. It's a privilege to meet you and of course Calico. I love cats. Although I must say I'm having trouble with your way of talking. Rachel." Skylar said.

"Ah the language, yes I haveth a spell for that. Each of us in this place must speaketh the language of this time not our own at least to thou ears. By BARALAMENSIS, BALDACHIENSIS, AND the most potent princes GENO, LIACHIDE, I command that all people of thine time shall hearest those of this time in their own language." Rachel said with a wave of her wand.

Calico spoke right after Rachel.

"By the way, nice to meet you girls. Of course, I like cat lovers better than ordinary people. You wouldn't believe how many people dislike us." Calico said.

"Am I crazy or did that Calico cat just speak to us and in our own modern dialect." Carly said her eyes wide with wonder.

"Of courses I did. I've been speaking since I was a kitten, although I must say I didn't make much sense then. The difference here is that you understand what I'm saying. In the real world, no person can speak the cat language. Oh and by the way my name is Calico not Calico cat." Calico said cocking his head upward.

"I know how most if not all the people came here but how did you come into the World In Between." Skylar asked.

"A long time ago in cat time but only forty years in your time, I hunted a bird on the lawn outside of the front fence of Tanglewood. I used my very best stealthy crawl. The robin never heard me coming. I pounced on the robin but before I could enjoy my catch, I heard loud barking and the pounding of heavy feet. A big black dog quickly closed on me. I dropped the robin and ran as fast as I could. I held my own for a while, but soon the dog gained on me. An oak tree grew right next to the fence at the entrance and I leaped for it just as the dog caught up to me. I could feel his jaws close inches from my tail. Fortunately, I grabbed a hold of the tree and rapidly climbed out of the dog's reach. Before I knew it I had climbed half way up the large tree. I waited in the tree until the dog grew tired of barking and left.

While I avoided almost certain death from the jaws of the dog, I couldn't climb down the tree. My owners took me to a doctor as a kitten and removed my front claws. I couldn't very well stay in the tree, so I climbed onto one of the large branches and walked all the way to the front gate on it. I saw a large number of locks on the gate and decided to do one of my famous cat leaps to reach the locks. I thought I could make the locks into kind of a ladder. I did so but I had difficulty holding on to the slippery cast iron fence, the cage over the locks and the wobbly locks. As I struggled to hold on, one of my backs claws went into the one of the locks' keyhole. I saw a flash of light and found myself standing right here. I've been here ever since. All the girls here took a liking to me as did Rachel, so I divide my time between them. That's pretty much it." Calico said.

"That's a neat story Calico. It's a privilege to talk with my first cat. I can see why your language is more like ours. You are only a little over forty, my dad's age." Carly said.

Rachel suddenly joined the conversation after a few quiet moments passed.

"You sayest distant relative. What year be it in the real world? Your clothes I knowest not."

"It's 2014 over two hundred years from the time you entered this place. I can't believe you and Elizabeth are still alive after all that time. Oh and Rachel, your language spell didn't work. You're still speaking as a woman from the seventeen hundreds." Carly said.

"That be impossible! I knowest we've been here a long time, but two hundred fifty years more. I have aged not a day. Oh and about the spell, which workest not. I remember not the gods, which are most high. By the Most Holy and glorious Names ADONAI, EL, ELOHIM, ELOHE, ZEBAOTH, ELION, ESCHERCE, JAH, TETRAGRAMMATON, SADAI and by BARALAMENSIS, BALDACHIENSIS, AND the most potent princes GENO, LIACHIDE, I command that people of this human time shall hearest thee residents of the Time in Between in the language that be their own." Rachel said.

"Are you really alive as you were when you came in here?" Constance asked Rachel when she finished her spell.

"Yes as far as I know. At least, I don't feel any different. You, however, don't look like your friends." Rachel said studying Constance.

"I'm not; I'm a ghost. I died in 1850, but have haunted the Worthington Mansion all this time. For some reason the magic in this place has made me visible. Oh and by the way, congratulations, your magic worked this time. You're speaking modern dialect which I have learned as a ghost by listening to the residents of the duke's house." Constance responded.

"Yes the magic here is extremely powerful, more so than I ever imagined. Even in the ancient texts I studied there is no mention of a spell lasting more than two hundred years and allowing cats to talk. Also, I could never get the spell I just cast on language translation to work before. Yet, even magic has its limits. I sense the spell Elizabeth and I created is weakening." Rachel said.

"Does that mean we can get out of here?" Carly asked.

"Yes, but the strange way time works in here may cause many years to pass in your world. You could loose fifty years in here before the spell collapses." Rachel responded.

"That won't do for any of us. We're just kids and want to continue to be kids. We even have boyfriends. Can you help us open the door so we can leave right away?" Skylar asked.

"Yes I can but I'll probably have to fight Elizabeth to do it. So I will make you this offer. I'll open the door if you take the keys with you. This spell has lasted too long. The kids trapped in here must be allowed to move onto whatever awaits them. Elizabeth and I need to move on as well. Only you girls can remove the keys as you came to this world of your own free will. You did not commit some act on the outside that put you here." Rachel responded.

"Okay it's a deal. How do we find the keys?" Carly asked.

"They're at the bottom of the Cave of Despair, which is visible from the top of the hill in front of you. The cave is a very scary place. Elizabeth placed many traps, spells and creatures in this dark place to keep people like you away." Rachel said.

"Great, this adventure of ours becomes more difficult by the minute, but I guess we don't have any choice. I don't want to come out of here and greet a sixty five year old Peter." Skylar said.

"Nor do I want to date a sixty five year old Cory. Rachel, is there anything we should know before we enter the cave?" Skylar said.

"No. I'm afraid I don't know very much about it. Since none of us can take the keys to the outside world, only one person has explored the cave." Rachel said.

"Rachel one more question. Where are all the kids trapped in here?" Carly asked.

"They can be found almost everywhere. You'll no doubt run into some of them on the way to the cave. They're all girls with the exception of the one boy who tampered with the lock trying to reach his girlfriend. He as you might well imagine receives a great deal of female attention. He might be the only person here who doesn't want this world to end." Rachel said with a smile forming on her face.

"Sounds like a boy," Carly said laughing.

"I'll see you soon. I have to see what Elizabeth is doing." Rachel said as she disappeared in the same way she had come.

The girls walked for several minutes after Rachel left but then Skylar suddenly turned to Carly.

"Carly you've been my best friend since the second grade. We used to read fairly tales together. This is no fairy tale. This place is real. We could actually die or be trapped here like the other key girls. There will be no fair prince to save us. I feel a little numb and very scared."

"I'm scared too Skylar, but our lives have been too sheltered until now. We're growing up and part of doing that is to face real risks, just as boys do when they go off to war. We'll be better people after this adventure."

"Yeah if we survive." Skylar said as she put her arm around Carly.

Inquisition

eggy and Jade walked slowly toward the headmistresses' office. They had been summoned for what they expected to be unpleasant questioning about their friends. Peggy spoke in a low voice.

"Peter and Cory keep e-mailing me. They're very worried about Skylar and Carly and want to know what to do. Rufus keeps e-mailing me as well concerned about the kind of punishment the school is going to give us. He is afraid we will get kicked out."

"Peter and Cory are copying me on their e-mails to you. Thad has the same worries as Rufus. He thinks we will be expelled and he will never see me again. At least, Cory and Thad explained to Rufus and Peter what actually happened. I don't think the headmistress will be willing to listen to the truth." Jade added.

"No she won't Jade. This is a real mess. Anyway, we're at the door. I don't see the headmistresses' secretary. I wonder if we should just walk into her office."

"I guess so Peggy."

Gathering all their courage, the two girls peeked around the door and saw Tabatha waving at them to come in. Tabatha sat alone as the girls walked inside her office. In a formal way, she addressed them.

"Please take a seat. A detective from the Sheriff's Department, Carly and Skylar's parents and our security chief will be joining us in fifteen minutes. Before they do, I need to discuss the punishment I will give you for lying to us. I also want to discuss any role you had in the disappearance of your friends. Before we start, your boyfriends at Briar Manor, Cory and Thad who accompanied you on this trip through our tunnels will be confined to campus for one-month because of the part they played in supporting your story and being in this school against our policy. They have admitted the six of you went into the tunnels but they haven't told us what happened to Carly and Skylar. They said the two of you should explain it. So please tell me the truth."

"We didn't tell you the truth because we thought you wouldn't believe us. We even feared you'd put us in a mental institution." Peggy said.

"Look I attended this school twenty five years ago. I know all about the Magic Keys legend. I even thought about looking for the magical world in the tunnels like my friends wanted to but I never did. I assume this is what you did as the key to the tunnel pad lock mysteriously disappeared. You may not know this but over one hundred girls have investigated those tunnels over the years. So whatever you say to me will not come as a big surprise." Tabatha said. Peggy and Jade looked at each other for several minutes and then after a few whispers and hand signals Jade answered Tabatha.

"Okay then we'll tell you. I didn't know that many girls had been in the tunnels but we're different than them. Skylar, Carly, Peggy, Cory, Thad and I actually found the magical World in Between where the keys are kept. Carly and Skylar went inside this world but the rest of us weren't allowed inside. I don't know why. It may have to do with their relatives being among the original girls who knew the evil witch Elizabeth. We made up the story we did to buy some time to go back there and rescue our friends, but you've watched us so closely we haven't been able to." Jade said.

"I'm sorry girls, I don't believe in magical worlds but I do believe that your friends became lost in the tunnels. You should have told us immediately so we could start searching for them. Do they have any food and water?"

"Yes they had both in their backpacks, but you won't find them in the tunnels no matter how hard you search." Peggy said.

"We'll just have to disagree on this point. I'm going to put off our discussion about where your friends are until the others arrive in just a few minutes. Maybe the detective can get more information out of you, but I'm certain everyone at that meeting will want to go to the tunnels and look for Carly and Skylar. As to your punishment for lying and perhaps not even telling us the whole truth even now, I'm going to give you the same punishment as your boyfriends received: one month restriction to campus unless you're supervised by an adult. Actually, you deserve a several month suspension but I owe you and your friends in the tunnels a big debt for the way you treated Betty. I don't know what you girls said to her but Betty started losing weight after talking to you and has been a much happier student as a result. Betty gives you all the credit. Frankly, Betty's parents and I worried that Betty might hurt herself. It kept me up nights. Betty threatened to do so several times. Still, I don't want you girls to think you have gotten away with what you just did with just a slap on the wrist. If you don't' help us find your friends, I might very well increase your punishment. Is that understood?" Tabatha said.

"Headmistress please believe us when we say that we want to find Skylar and Carly as much as you do. They're our best friends. As to Betty, we're very happy she is feeling better. Girls obsess too much about their weight. We tried to tell Betty that she wasn't alone in struggling with this problem." Jade said.

"I guess she listened to you. Anyway, I hear the rest of our guests in the hall. Why don't you tell Detective Stevens what you just told me and any other details that might help."

Detective Stevens, Bert, Skylar's and Carly's mothers and fathers, and Tanglewood's security chief walked into the room staring at Peggy and Jade. Before Peggy, Jade or Tabatha could say anything the detective spoke.

"Ladies your story about where your friends went just doesn't hold up even though you managed to persuade your boyfriends to back up your lies. If anyone knows where they went, you do. You may have sworn to your friends to keep their secret but by doing so you have put their lives in danger. The world can be a very mean place for young innocent girls like your friends. Now tell us what you know--the truth this time."

Peggy spoke. "Detective we just told Tabatha what happened. We did mislead you a little but we did so because we didn't think you'd accept the truth. You'd call us crazy. Frankly, when I think of what happened, I still can't believe it."

"Detective this whole thing is about the Magic Keys legend which is part of the folklore at this school from its earliest days in the middle of the 18th century. One of the first students at this school, a witch named Elizabeth supposedly put one girl every year into a magical world at Halloween because the daughter of the duke who founded this school teased her. When she did, a lock appeared on our front gate. When you drove in here your probably saw these locks hanging on the fence behind an iron cage. These disappearances continued for several years until Elizabeth and another witch were drawn into this magic world after a fight. Girls stopped disappearing after that but according to the legend the lost girls are forever locked in this strange world until the keys to the locks are found and used to open them. Almost every year, girls search our tunnels looking for this magic world and the keys it contains. Thad, Cory, Skylar, Carly, Peggy and Jade joined this long line of kids looking for the keys but unlike all that have gone before, claim to have found this magic world in the tunnels. According to them, Skylar and Carly disappeared into this world but the rest of them weren't allowed into it. Most of us don't believe that this World in Between and its magic keys exist. Still the legend persists. Its part of the tradition and allure of the school."

"With all due respect to your school and your legends, this is utter nonsense. I don't believe any of it. I can see, however, how four young girls and two of their boyfriends could believe it and make a dangerous trip into some old tunnels. Then I can see two of the girls becoming trapped or hurt down there. Is that what happened?" The detective said staring at Jade and Peggy.

"No as far as we know Carly and Skylar aren't hurt at least they weren't when we last saw them. Through magic we dissolved the shimmering shield protecting the World In Between. Then Skylar and Carly opened the oak door and went inside this world. We tried to follow them but a new invisible wall the witch created kept us from entering. Then the oak door swung shut and locked us outside. We couldn't get through two barriers. We tried but failed. We decided we needed magic to get in the door and to lower the second shield but don't know what kind of magic it will take." Jade answered.

"Did Carly and Skylar have any food or water?" Skylar's father Bill asked.

"Yes. Each of us had a backpack with food, water and flashlights. I had the biggest back pack with the magic supplies in addition to the food and water." Jade answered not mentioning that Thad carried her backpack most of the way.

"At this point, it doesn't really make any difference whether this story is true or not. Those girls are somewhere down in those tunnels. We have to find them now. We haven't any time to lose. You girls should have told us about this place as soon as your friends went missing. Take us to the place you last saw your friends." Bert said.

"Okay but it won't do you any good. You have to use magic to enter the World In Between." Peggy said.

Search Party

After everyone rose, the detective, the four parents, and the Tanglewood security officer followed Jade and Peggy out the door and down to the basement. The headmistress needed to stay at her desk and handle Tanglewood business, which now included press inquiries about the missing girls. Jade and Peggy tried to whisper to each other but the adults stayed so close to them that they had trouble understanding what each other said. Both Jade and Peggy felt trapped. They didn't want to lead these adults to the secret passageway and the entrance to the World In-Between but they didn't feel they had any choice in the matter. The headmistress had already mentioned they might be suspended from the school. Clearly, the adults wanted to blame them for the disappearance of Carly and Skylar. They needed to be as cooperative as possible.

When the search party reached the southeast corner of the tunnels, Jade and Peggy looked for the rock they left. They found it but clearly it had moved a little. Fortunately, they had scratched the walls next to the door release. Carefully moving away from the rock along the wall to the right, they found the scratches. The adults looked on in shock when Peggy pulled the lever, which moved more easily this time and the secret door swung open. As soon as the door opened, all of them could hear the faint noises, feel the air tingling, and smell the sewer like odor, but Peggy and Jade noticed all three had grown weaker since they last visited. Jade decided to tell everyone about the tunnel.

"Skylar's great, many greats, grandfather the duke built this tunnel between his house and Tanglewood, which was his sister's house at the time, to hide from both colonial and royal soldiers during the Revolutionary War. He hid it so well very few people knew of its existence. A girl named Debbie who went to Tanglewood in the 1840's found out about it and correctly concluded that the corridor to the World in Between branched off of it. Many years later another girl Sandra found Debbie's diary. She used it to find the entrance to the World in Between but decided not to try and enter it. The corridor is about a hundred yards from here."

Skylar's father Edward spoke next.

"This is incredible. My family has always known about this tunnel, but could never find it on our end. Of course, that doesn't mean that the World in Between exists, but it's still impressive that you found the tunnel."

"Even though we were all involved, your daughter probably had the most to do with finding it." Peggy said.

"That sounds like her. I have to say that this odor, noise and tingling sensation are very curious. I still don't believe in the World in Between but I can't explain these phenomena." Edward said.

The group walked slowly along calling out to Skylar and Carly. They received no answer only the echo of their own voices. After ten minutes of walking, Jade saw the special corridor and quickly addressed the rest of the party with concern in her voice.

"The corridor is there but it looks like the corridor had a cave in. All I can say is that those rocks blocking the corridor weren't there two days ago."

Detective Stevens carefully examined the rocks and debris blocking the corridor. He noticed how much stronger the smells, noises, and tingling sensation was in the spaces between the rocks. He finally said.

"This cave in is very recent. Some of the dust from the collapse is still in the air. We are going to have to bring some equipment in to move some of the large rocks but I think we can working together move some of the smaller ones. It may give us enough room to pass. All of you who know Carly and Skylar please call to them. They may be trapped behind this debris."

"Let's please hurry. Our daughter could be hurt in there." Mary the mother of Carly said.

All the adults called for Skylar and Carly through the small holes in the blocked corridor but once again they received no response. Jade and Peggy did not call to their friends knowing that they couldn't hear them. Working hard for a half hour, the search party managed to move much of the debris and some of the smaller rocks but the big rocks and chunks of the wall needed as the detective said heavy equipment to move. Everyone noticed that the smells, sounds and tingling sensation became much stronger with part of the blockage removed. Although a little treacherous, the search party had cleared a large enough opening for people to move into the corridor. The youngest and smallest of the group, Jade and Peggy easily moved into the corridor and helped the rest of the party reach the other side. When the party shone their lights down the corridor, they immediately saw the shimmering barrier.

"I can't believe I'm looking at this. Is there military research taking place around here? This barrier looks like something out of a science fiction movie. Maybe we can put our hands on it or walk through it." Bill, Carly's dad, said.

"We tried that. The wall burns you very badly if you come in contact with it. It's every bit as dangerous as it looks." Jade said.

Detective Stevens stared at the barrier for several minutes; then called out to the rest of the party.

"Okay if we can't come in contact with it, I have another idea. Lie down on the floor. I'm going to fire my gun at the barrier. If there is a ricochet I don't want anyone getting hurt. Also, put your hands over your ears. This gun may be very loud in here."

The detective fired his gun at the shield but nothing happened. The bullet did not ricochet as feared but seemed to disappear into the shield. The detective shaking his head fired seven more shots into the shield but as before nothing happened. The shimmering wall remained. Gazing at the spell materials on the floor of the corridor, Detective Stevens said.

"You used that stuff to lower the shield or whatever it is?"

"Yeah we did. When we left the area, the shield or shimmering wall returned." Peggy replied.

"Detective, my daughter is in there. She might be hurt. Let the girls try to lower the shield again. Even if they fail, there is no harm in them trying." Mary said.

"Okay. What do we need to do to help?" The detective said.

With the adults help, the girls quickly prepared the pentagram. Fortunately, Skylar left the paper with the spell on it behind when she walked into the world in between. They did, however, have to dig up some moist soil nearby. They already used the soil that came with the kit. The girls decided that this soil would be more effective than the kit soil as it came from this place of magic. Also, having more people chant the magic words should give the spell more power or at least the girls hoped so.

When everyone sat in a circle, Jade read the evocation part of the spell then waving her hand in the air, the entire group said the magic words: Se Dissolvant Claustrum Falsa five times. As before, nothing happened at first then suddenly the wall dissolved. The entire group walked quickly past the barrier to the large oak door. The detective tried the door, but couldn't budge it. Then the security guard and the two fathers started to pull on the door as well. The door did not move. The detective put another ammunition clip in his revolver and once again asked everyone to move back. Firing eight shots into the door he literally shredded the area around the doorknob but the door still refused to open. The gun did, however, make a hole in the door large enough for everyone to look at the World in Between beyond. Each person took a turn looking except the girls who looked before.

The security guard Ted who had remained quiet for most of the trip spoke first.

"I'm having a very hard time believing my eyes. This must be some kind of dream. Shimmering walls don't exist; neither do fuzzy worlds with strange vibrant colors. Did someone put some drugs in the water we drank?"

"No I don't think so. I don't feel drugged. Look, I'm trained to look at facts. The shimmering wall exists. We all saw it. So does the weird world beyond this wall. Once again we all saw it. If we were hallucinating we wouldn't all see the same thing. What we don't know is how or why these things are here. We have this witch story, which I quite frankly think is absurd, but I have to admit that silly spell lowered the wall. According to Jade and Peggy, the lost girls are in that strange world there. So, I guess we have one and only one thing we can do. We must open this door and go after them." Detective Stevens said trying to make something logical, which defied logic.

Ted, the security guard immediately started rummaging through the long pack he brought with him. He spoke as he did so.

"I brought an axe and some heavy lock cutters. I though we might need one or both to get through some old and rusted doors in these tunnels. These tools were of no use in the cave in but the axe is just what we need here. I'll start chopping up the door. When I get tired, the rest of you can have your turn. The door is pretty heavy but we should be able to open a hole large enough to crawl through in a half hour or so."

"Good thinking. I'll be sure to say good things about you to the headmistress. I'll gladly take the next turn. If that door is all that is stopping us we need to get rid of it as soon as we can." Edward said.

Forty-five minutes later, all the male adults sweated heavily. Edward panted more heavily than the rest, worrying all of them. They managed to open up a hole in the door large enough for all of them to crawl through to the other side but the badly mangled door still refused to move. Once again Jade and Peggy, the smallest of the group, offered to go first. They made it through the door without a problem but as they did so, both ran into the invisible wall. They shook their heads and moved out of the hole in the door. Several adults also tried to enter the strange world but also ran into the wall. Finally, the security chief waved everyone away and starting swinging at the invisible barrier with his axe. The axe struck the invisible wall with a loud clang but did no apparent damage to it. One again each adult swung the axe, but the invisible barrier showed no visible sign of being struck. Finally, Bill said.

"Girls, what are we going to do now?"

"I don't know. Elizabeth the evil witch put the new wall there after Skylar and Carly entered. She knew we could move beyond her shimmering barrier and chop down the door." Jade said.

"Will the spell that worked on the shimmering wall work on this invisible wall?" Edward asked.

"I suppose we could try. Let's move all the materials next to it." Peggy said.

The group did so. Once again they carefully recreated the spell to dissolve the door but after they said the magic words, nothing happened. The invisible door remained. The group tried a second time but once again the wall remained. Peggy commented.

"Obviously we need a different spell for this invisible wall but I've no idea what kind of spell that might be. Skylar knew the most about this magic stuff. Jade and I don't really know anything beyond what Skylar showed us."

Frustrated the detective said.

"We aren't accomplishing anything. We need to bring some contractors down here with heavy equipment. The front wall may not fall but the sidewalls don't have a spell protecting them. Maybe we can get into this strange world that way. "

"Do whatever you have to do but bring my daughter back!" Edward said. The other adults nodded their heads in agreement.

Meeting the Key Girls

After Skylar, Constance, Carly and Calico who had decided to join them walked over the hill, they began seeing girls their own age. A blonde hailed them.

"I don't believe I know you. Your clothes are very strange. Who are you?"

"My name is Skylar; this is my good friend Carly and my distant relative Constance. Carly and I live in what you probably think of as the distant future. In truth, in the real world, it's 2014. Our world is very advanced compared to the world in which you lived. Constance died in an 1850 world not that much different than your own. She is a ghost that can appear here because of the powerful magic in this place."

"I'm Cynthia and I came to this place in 1763. What you say is incredible to me. I actually believe in ghosts but I never thought I'd see one. As to the date, I knew we had been here a long time but over two hundred fifty years! This is very hard for me to accept. Everyone I knew not in here is long since dead. No one even remembers them. No one remembers me."

"I'm sorry Cynthia this happened to you. We came here to get the magic keys and put an end to this long curse that has imprisoned you. According to Rachel, we can do that because the curse didn't bring us in here. Anything you know about the keys would be a great help. Rachel already told us that the keys are at the bottom of the cave and that the cave is full of scary traps and creatures." Carly said.

"Yes, Rachel, who we call the good witch, is telling the truth. We know that because Beatrice who came here in 1765 made it to the bottom of the cave and saw the keys. She is the only one who ever did so. I'd recommend you find her and ask her to accompany you. She knows where all the traps and creatures are. I think she is as anxious as I am to get out of here. Still, I should caution you. Elizabeth, who we call the evil witch, will try to stop you. She can be very mean." Cynthia said.

"Actually, she brought us in here and put some kind of spell on the door so we couldn't get out. If we have the keys, maybe we can use their magic to get us out of here. At least, I hope we can." Skylar said.

"It's certainly worth a try. I'll accompany you until we find Beatrice and maybe even into the cave, but answer me a question first. What will happen to us when the keys are put in the locks? We're supposed to return to the real world but we've been here so long we might die the moment we leave here." Cynthia worried.

"I don't know. Maybe Rachel does. Still, whatever happens, you'll be returning to the world in which you belong. I've been dead a long time. I know there is a beautiful world in the light that appears to dead people. If you go there, it won't be bad at all of that I am sure. If all of you go into the light, I may even join you. In any case, this cursed world is not the right place for any of you to be." Constance said.

"In that we agree. If they had a place for the insane in here, I think we would all be there. It's torture to spend endless days here. There is absolutely nothing to do. There are only a few books, no school, and nothing with which to play. Only one boy is here and he came here to be with his girlfriend. Even after all these years, he is still with her. Can you imagine living more than two hundred years without a man or boy in your life? We are almost never hungry and never have to go to the bathroom. It's like being frozen but still moving. I don't even know what I am anymore. In a sense I'm still a kid and in another sense I'm an old woman. " Cynthia said.

"We're here to put a stop to this curse. More than two hundred years is enough time to get even for a grudge. So let's go find this Beatrice." Carly said.

Without further conversation, the four girls and Calico walked past the cave into the farthest reaches of the strange in between world. They met many of the girls entrapped there including the one boy and

Tiffany. A new resident, Tiffany still seemed confused about the World in Between.

"I keep pinching myself, thinking that this place has to be a bad dream, but when I do, I'm still here. It has to be impossible. It just has to be."

"Carly and I are from the present like you and believe me, this place is very real. We're going to get you out of here. We will." Skylar said.

"Thank you. My dad and mom must be worried sick thinking some man abducted me or some other terrible thing happened to me. I should have never messed around with that magic lock."

"If you don't make it out, we'll tell them where you really are but you're going to make it along with the rest of the girls here." Carly said with some confidence.

The girls continued to walk through the magic world until they came upon Samantha the original inhabitant and the one responsible for creating the curse. After Cynthia introduced the girls, Skylar addressed her very distant cousin, who appeared a little depressed.

"I never thought I would have an opportunity of meeting the daughter of the duke and the person so involved in creating the Magic Keys of Tanglewood myth. As your distant relative and inhabitant of the mansion your father built, I feel connected to you. Even for those Tanglewood girls not related to you, you've fired their imaginations for hundreds of years, even the ones now living in our world of 2014."

"It's nice to meet a distant relative who still lives on our estate. I never thought our family would still be living in our ancestral home after all this time. My father really built a legacy that lasted. Before you ask, yes I'm very sorry that I caused all the trouble that led to this terrible curse. I acted like a bully and all these people in here with me have had to pay the price for my actions. I'm not that girl anymore but despite my best efforts I haven't been able to convince Elizabeth of how sorry I am. You're the first girls to come here in a very long time. What is your purpose?" Samantha asked.

"As we told Cynthia we're here to retrieve the keys, take them to the fence where the locks still hang and open all the locks bringing this terrible curse to an end. Cynthia is taking us to find Beatrice. She can reportedly help us locate the keys at the bottom of the cave. Oh and

Rachel said we can take the keys out of here as we came in here of our own free will." Carly said.

"Just because you can walk out of here with the keys doesn't mean Elizabeth will let you. She lives off this curse and the misery it has brought all of us." Samantha said.

"We'll confront Elizabeth when the time comes. I have a few things to say to her. Maybe the good witch Rachel will help us. Any way as my dad often says sometimes you just have to take on challenges even though the odds of success aren't great. So are you ready for a challenge? Do you want to come"? Skylar asked. Samantha stared at the girls in the strange outfits who stood before her for almost two minutes before she answered.

"Maybe I should. Maybe we all should. She'll have trouble fighting all of us. It's time. Anyway what can she do to us that she hasn't already done to us? I'll ring the general meeting bell." Samantha said surprising herself.

Constance, Skylar, Carly, Calico and Cynthia stood there in amazement as all the people trapped in the world in between gathered around the bell. Beatrice came along with the others. Samantha held up her hand.

"The time has come to put an end to this curse and this place. These girls from the present, which will surprise you is 2014, intend to walk out of here with the keys. They can do so because the curse didn't bring them here. The only way they will succeed is if we all stand against Elizabeth together. If you think about it, there is nothing Elizabeth can do to us she hasn't already done. We need to join the real world either as spirits or live people."

"Elizabeth's traps are terrible and frightening as are her creatures. I barely made it out of the cave in one piece. I swore never to return to that cave after failing to collect the keys. Now you're asking all of us to go there." Beatrice said.

"Alright what if the traps or creatures killed you there. What would happen? I'm a ghost. I already died. There is another wonderful world in the light that appears to every dead person. This world is part of the normal order of things unlike this place, which is an abomination. You would be much better off there than here. If you aren't killed, you might be able to return to the modern world and enjoy the life you never had." Constance said.

"If this world in the light is so wonderful why didn't you go there?" Beatrice persisted.

"Because I loved the my house and wanted to stay there. I've always known that I would eventually go into the light. Maybe if all of you go into the light, I'll go too." Constance responded.

"That's good enough for me. I'm going with these outsiders. The more of us that go the better chance we have of winning. Any way, these outsiders are the only ones with anything at risk. This is their time. If they die on this quest, it's as if someone killed them in the real world. They will leave loved ones behind. All our loved ones are long since dead." Cynthia said.

The girls and one boy stood for several minutes; then slowly began nodding their heads. Not wanting the mood to change, Skylar immediately started marching back down the road toward the cave. Without comment, every one else followed her. These girls and boy had never acted together this way before.

Skylar suddenly turned toward Carly.

"Carly I'm afraid again. I thought when we talked about this before I had put my fear behind me. But I haven't. Samantha is right. We're the ones here taking all the risks."

"Me too. As a little girl, I thought that a monster lived in my closest. I dreamed about the creature all the time. I refused to go to sleep many nights until late. I turned ten before I finally overcame my fear of the closest creature. I feel like I did then. I guess if we die we have Constance to help us. We won't be alone. At least that's something." Carly responded.

"Will you take care of us Constance?" Skylar asked.

"Yes of course. You're my friends and Skylar you're my blood. I'll be there for you."

Skylar nodded as did Carly. Then, they fell strangely silent. The group with Beatrice now in the lead slowly moved toward the cave. In about ten minutes, they reached it. Elizabeth suddenly appeared before them, anger and rage covering her face.

"Where do you think you're going? My traps and creatures will kill every one of you! I stopped Beatrice last time and I'll stop you this time."

"We aren't afraid of you anymore. These outsiders are going to help us get out of here. Whatever debt I or anyone else had to you is long since paid." Samantha said.

Elizabeth rose to her full height and pulled out her wand almost screaming.

"Your debt will never be paid! I'll confine you here for all of eternity."

After yelling at Samantha. Elizabeth pointed her wand at Skylar and Carly and said.

"I'll take care of you invaders of my world."

With her wand moving through the air in a tight circle, Elizabeth started mumbling a spell but before she could complete it, Rachel suddenly appeared and snatched the wand out of her hand.

"No you don't. This needs to end." Rachel said.

Elizabeth just stared at Rachel and then at all the inhabitants of her world. She finally said.

"This isn't over. The traps, spells and creatures in the cave will kill most of you. I'll kill whoever is left when you come out of the cave."

When no one responded to her, Elizabeth disappeared as suddenly as she appeared.

"Even though I told Elizabeth how sorry I felt for bullying her all those years ago, I still don't like her. She seems to like being mean." Samantha said.

Beatrice walked to the front of the procession and spoke.

"Samantha you're right about Elizabeth and that's why we need to be smart about how we approach this quest. All of us don't have to go into the cave. I need to go because I know the way, the outsiders need to go as they maybe the only ones that can handle the keys, and maybe Cynthia and Samantha should go as well. The rest of you need to guard the cave entrance and keep Elizabeth away."

The one boy Terrance spoke.

"You need a man on this trip. Elizabeth always treats me differently than she does the rest of you."

"Alright, I guess that makes sense." Beatrice said.

"Wait a minute-my boyfriend doesn't go anywhere without me. Beatrice and Cynthia both of you have been trying to get your hands on Terrance for a long time." Barbara, Terrance's girlfriend said.

"I guess that's alright but I think that is enough people. Are we ready?" Samantha added.

"Wait a minute. That certainly is enough people, but you need a cat like me with my better sense of smell and hearing. Cats are born hunters." Calico said.

"Okay Calico you can come. If we have to face creatures and animals you will be a big help." Beatrice said.

The large group of people at the cave entrance all nodded their heads. The quest group consisting of Calico, Carly, Skylar, Constance, Samantha, Beatrice, Cynthia, Terrance, and Barbara headed toward the entrance. Beatrice suddenly stopped and turned toward Rachel.

"Rachel what are you going to do?"

"I'll stay close to the cave entrance and watch for Elizabeth. If she becomes aggressive like she did a few minutes ago, I'll stop her. I have her wand. Without it she can't do much. Still, I'm having a hard time holding onto it. Elizabeth has the power to make her wand fly back to her the moment I take my hand off of it." Rachel replied.

"That makes sense." Turning to the rest of the quest group, Beatrice continued speaking. "Follow me. I remember where each trap is located. Still, we have to be careful. Elizabeth might have moved the traps."

The Cave

kylar, Constance and Carly immediately noticed that the smell, noise and tingling sensation they felt when they came to this world became much stronger in the cave. They farther they descended in the cave the stronger these sensations. The cave seemed to be the heart of this strange world. As frightening as the cave seemed to the quest group, a very faint light filled it. They could all see if they looked very carefully. Still, the deeper they went into the cave the fainter the light. Skylar spoke to the group about the light issue.

"Carly has an electric lantern and I have a flashlight. Most of you don't know what they are but they provide light. We'll turn them on when it becomes too dark in here."

"Its already too dark and scary in here. Turn them on now." Cynthia said.

"They run on batteries which can wear out. I don't want the batteries to fail before we reach the keys. Still, don't worry. Carly and I will be turning the lights on very soon." Skylar said.

Moments after Skylar spoke, Beatrice held up her hand.

"The first trap is somewhere close to here. It's a cleverly hidden hole in the ground, which descends into a swirling red space. You can't see the bottom. It's covered by a thin layer of dust on a very rotten piece of wood, so you won't see it until you fall through. Let's walk in a single file."

The group dutifully lined up that way and followed Beatrice. Barbara, however, didn't follow the line very carefully, wandering off to the left a little. Her left foot suddenly fell through the rotten board over the hole. Barbara began to fall into the hole, shrieking at the top of her lungs, but at the last moment, Skylar who walked nearby grabbed her hand and pulled her back onto the path. They all stared at the frightening hole and the red light that came from it. Barbara barely able to speak managed to say to Skylar.

"Thanks for saving me. I didn't want to die this way. I'm shaking all over my body."

"You're welcome. We're all in this together. Anyway, I think you've convinced me we need more light." Skylar replied as she turned on her flashlight. Carly standing next to Skylar turned on her much brighter lantern moments after Skylar turned on her flashlight. The quest teams suddenly saw the cave in the detail they missed before.

The cave had smooth gray walls. Most of the wall seemed to be dry but patches of the wall showed some moisture. The ground consisted of dust and fine rocks but as with the walls showed some wet spots. The ground up ahead sloped downward but in some places the ground appeared to be almost flat while in others the ground seemed to be steep. They approached a steep area right now, which they hadn't been aware of prior to the lights being turned on. Samantha couldn't help but comment.

"Those lanterns aren't burning. I can't smell any wax or whale oil. What is a battery and how can they throw off so much light without burning?"

"It's about electricity, which is part of almost everything in my world. Constance should know a little about it. I think they had telegraphs in her time, which use electricity."

"Yes we just started using telegraphs, but we didn't have anything like these wondrous lights." Constance replied.

"Now that we have light we need to go. Despite our friends at the cave entrance, I worry about facing Elizabeth in here." Beatrice said.

"Okay lead on." Carly responded.

At just this moment, Calico arched her back and growled.

"Calico what is it?" Beatrice said.

"I smell bear. I don't know where he came from but he is walking down the path behind us. I'll hold him off while you walk farther down the path."

"Calico you can't confront a bear by yourself. He'll kill you." Samantha said.

"I have a plan, now please hurry. Although very large and bulky, bears can move very quickly." Calico whispered.

The party without Calico moved several meters down the path and waited. They heard the distinct growl of the bear and suddenly the huge creature reared back on his hindquarters and tried to swipe Calico with first his right and then his left paw. Calico leaped backwards, barely avoiding the bears' long claws. Angry now, the bear chased Calico where he intended the bear to chase him right toward the large hole. As Calico reached the hole, the bear caught Calico with a left swipe sending him crashing into the wall, but the powerful swing caused the bear to loose his balance at the rim of the hole. Despite the bear's best efforts to avoid the hole, he toppled forward into it, frantically scratching the hole's walls in an attempt to stop his fall. The heavy bear could not stop his fall and grunting and bellowing disappeared into the holes' depths.

The search party ran to Calico who breathed heavily with a big gash in his side.

Skylar cried as she tried to comfort Calico.

"Calico, you're a true hero. You saved us from the bear, but you're badly hurt. I don't know what we can do to save you."

"Nothing, I'm dying. Just pet me in my final moments. I'd like to purr one last time." Calico said through his labored breath.

Skylar slowly pet Calico's uninjured areas and Calico purred for a few seconds then fell silent.

Skylar slowly lifted Calico and placed him near the wall. She spoke to the rest of the group.

"We will bury Calico when we leave and give him the honor he deserves."

"I'd appreciate that. I'm a hunter and represent a long tradition of brave cats that have gone before me. "Calico said appearing next to Constance as a ghost.

Just after Calico's ghost spoke, his body began to glow. The glow increased in intensity until seconds later Calico's body turned into dust and ash.

"That was very strange. I'm sorry Calico, we can't bury your body but I guess we can still bury your ashes. At least now, Constance you'll have a constant companion. Calico, that somehow makes me feel better about you dying in the horrible way you did." Samantha said.

"I'm okay, burying my ashes will be fine. Having Constance as a friend will make it much better for me in this strange spirit world I now occupy. In any case, we have a quest to complete. Let's go." Calico said.

"Before we do, I have a question of anyone who can answer it. Why didn't the bear appear as a spirit with Calico?" Carly asked.

"I don't think the bear ever existed outside the World In Between. Elizabeth created him to guard this cave. That didn't make him any less frightening or dangerous but since he didn't exist in the real world he had no soul." Beatrice answered.

"Thanks Beatrice, that makes sense. At least we don't have to worry about these creatures after they die." Carly said with a slight nod.

The quest team waving to Calico resumed their journey down the steep incline. Almost at the bottom, they heard another loud growl up ahead. They hesitated. Terrance spoke.

"I recognize that growl. It's a wolf. He can smell us. I bet Elizabeth put him in here to back up the bear. Wolves usually attack when they're hungry, but in this place people and I guess animals rarely eat. If they are girl dogs they will also attack if they have puppies to protect."

"I don't know if that makes any difference. Something is bothering that wolf. The wolf sounds very mad. Maybe Elizabeth messed with its mind as she likely did with the bear's mind." Skylar said.

"It doesn't matter. We need to continue and deal with the wolf when we have to do so. I can tell you that this wolf is new to the cave. I didn't encounter a wolf last time or the bear for that matter." Beatrice said.

After Beatrice began walking back down the cave path, the others followed. As they went, the growling grew louder. Still, the quest team walked forward. Then all of a sudden a huge wolf jumped in front of them. The wolf bared its teeth, its saliva dripping onto the ground. Carly immediately looked toward Terrance and said.

"Terrance give me your walking stick. We don't have a hole to swallow the wolf but I've an idea. "

Terrance did so. Carly walked to the front of the group and directly confronted the wolf. She spoke to Beatrice on her right and Samantha on her left.

"When the wolf leaps at me hold onto me and don't let me fall. The wolf gains the advantage if I'm on my back."

Carly stared into the red eyes of the snarling wolf and pointed the walking stick at the wolf. Despite some aggressive moves by the wolf, Carly did not move. For a moment, Carly believed that the wolf wouldn't attack, but when the attack came, it happened so swiftly that Carly didn't anticipate it. On second the wolf stood there; the next it leaped at her. At the last moment, Carly shoved the walking stick into the wolf's snarling mouth. The wolf's momentum forced the walking stick down its throat, but also brought the heavy animal onto Carly's chest. With her friends hanging on, Carly moved backward from the impact but did not fall. The wolf, however, did fall to the ground, writhing, shaking its head, snapping its jaws and backing away in an attempt to dislodge or break the walking stick. Carly using all her strength kept pushing the walking stick forward following the wolf's movement backward. The heavy oak walking stick did not break. In little over two minutes, the wolf rolled onto its back. Its movements slowed then stopped. The wolf's eyes turned glassy. After waiting another two minutes, Carly slowly removed the stick from the wolf's mouth. The wolf didn't move. As the people before him, the wolf turned to ash and dust. Shocked, Samantha spoke directly to Carly.

"You killed the wolf, but how did you know about shoving the stick into its mouth that way?"

"In our time, we have something called movies and television. Basically, a machine allows people to take moving pictures of what is around them. Then, the show or movie can be played back on a flat glass box. I don't really know enough about it to explain how this works, but it does. I watched on this flat glass box a show about how outdoors people fought dangerous animals in the forest. A man did this same thing I did with his arm when a wolf attacked him. His arm bled from some bites but the wolf, unable to breath died just as this wolf died. I decided to use the walking stick just as the man on television used his arm. I don't know if I would have had the courage to use my arm. Look at the walking stick. It has a number of holes in it from the wolf's teeth. I didn't want my arm to look that way. Terrance I'm sorry your walking stick isn't quite the way it was when you gave it to me but I think it'll still work."

"The walking stick is still fine for my needs. I had it with me when the curse brought me in here. I'm not sure I understand all your talk about movies and television, but I do know that you're a very brave girl. Not many people would have had the courage to face that huge angry wolf. I see you have some scratches on your chest just below your neck. Are you alright?" Terrance replied.

"Yes the scratches are only minor. They hurt but aren't bleeding very much." Carly replied.

"I think we're all grateful to Carly but we need to move ahead. The keys still wait for us at the bottom of the cave." Beatrice said as she turned to walk down the path. The rest of the group followed but all looked at Carly in a different way. They

admired her courage.

The cave continued to grow darker as they descended, but the lantern and flashlight gave them plenty of light. A very strong smell enveloped them. The quest team also sensed some movement above them. Cynthia suddenly broke the silence.

"I know that smell. Those are bats. We used to have some in a cave near our house. But as far as I know they are completely harmless. They eat fruit and insects."

"Unfortunately, these bats are different. I ran into them last time. They have big sharp teeth and like to bite animals and suck their blood." Beatrice said.

"They're Vampire Bats, but that makes no sense. They live in South America not here. Elizabeth must have somehow brought them to the cave. They do drink blood. We will have to be careful." Carly said.

"You know a great deal. I hope you have a way of killing these bats as you did the wolf." Samantha said.

"Yes, I have another idea if the bats attacks us. Let's hope they don't." Carly said.

The quest team walked cautiously forward under the bats flapping and moving above them. Their bat droppings, guano, smelled very bad and squished beneath their feet as they walked. The activity of the bats increased. Everyone knew they would attack soon. Carly waved to Constance and she floated over to her.

Carly whispered to Constance.

"Float to that spot away from us. Take Calico with you. When I give the signal, scream at your highest possible pitch. Ask Calico to meow at his highest pitch too. Bats use high frequency sounds. If your ghostly screams are high enough they should be attracted to them. I intend to put bat guano on different places on my body so I will smell more like a bat. I just hope it works. We have no way of fighting hundreds of flying bats with sharp teeth."

When Carly began to put bat guano on the various parts of her body, the rest of the quest team followed her lead. Samantha commented while holding her nose.

"Wow that smells really bad."

"A little smell won't hurt us but those teeth sure will." Skylar answered.

Just when Barbara the last one in the quest team finished covering her body, the bats suddenly flew off the ceiling in large numbers. Carly waved her arm at Constance. As Carly hoped, Constance's ghostly scream and Calico's meow registered very high on the pitch scale. Carly and the rest of the quest team couldn't hear any of it. The bats, however, heard it very well and attacked Constance and Calico with their sharp teeth. Of course, since Constance and Calico had no physical form as such, the bats snapped at mostly air. Some of the bats swooped down on the quest team but when they smelled the guano turned away at the last moment. Carly yelled to the rest of the team.

"Run!"

The quest team didn't need much encouragement. They quickly descended farther into the cave. The bats followed them for a while but then turned back toward the cave entrance. Just before the quest team reached the bottom, which spread out into a large cavern, Beatrice yelled, "Stop!"

The entire team stopped just before they entered the cavern. Beatrice addressed them.

"Elizabeth has buried spears and arrows in these walls ahead of us. If you step on one of the levers hidden in the ground, they come out of the walls with considerable force. You will probably be killed or wounded by them. The first lever is only inches from my front foot. They're ten of these levers in the next ten meters. I triggered one of the arrows last time. It missed me by centimeters. After the near miss, I spent almost an hour carefully making my way through the levers. I made a map of the levers and committed as much of my route to memory as I could. I will go first. The next in line will follow exactly in my footsteps as will everyone else. If you carefully follow my footsteps you'll be alright."

Beatrice slowly and quietly walked through the dangerous ten meters in front of them. Everyone carefully followed her lead. Barbara followed last. She had her eyes glued on Terrance in front of her. When Beatrice reached the end of the traps, a solitary bat, which somehow became separated from the rest of his flock, flew right into Barbara. Fighting off the bat, Barbara lost her balance. She had to put her foot out to the left to avoid falling. Barbara's left foot hit one of the levers. Terrance turned around but before he could help Barbara a spear flew out of the right wall into her chest. Terrance moved to help her, but Barbara put up her hand.

"No my love, stay where your are. I don't want you to die too. I love you and have always loved you. I'm sorry I won't be able to return to the real world with you. I….." Barbara stopped talking in mid sentence. Her eyes stared off into space and then she collapsed.

Terrance started to cry and moan.

"We should never have come here. We made a big mistake. Barbara didn't have to die. We could have live on as we have always done."

Barbara appearing next to Constance and Calico answered Terrance.

"No Terrance, coming here was and is the right thing to do. We couldn't stay in this awful place any longer. I admit dying hurt, but I feel free as a spirit. When we leave this place, I'll be able to go into the light and into a better place. I might even see my relatives there. I have Constance and Calico here to teach me about being a ghost. I'll be fine."

"Barbara, maybe I should step on another lever and join you." A tearful Terrance said.

"No, you need to help the rest of the quest team find and retrieve the magic keys. When the keys are returned to the real world you can join me in death if you want." Barbara replied.

"I'll do that, I promise I will." Terrance said sadly turning back toward the Cavern.

Right after Barbara appeared as a ghost, her body began to glow just as Calico's did. As the glow became brighter, Barbara's body started to slowly turn into ash and dust. Within a few minutes, only Barbara's ashes and dust remained. Samantha spoke first.

"What are we? I guess we aren't spirits as Barbara and Calico turned into one when they died, but bodies in the real world don't disintegrate like that. Like this place, we're different than real people."

"I don't know if you're different or just this place is different. If you think about it, everyone's body eventually turns to dust. Here, the process happens quickly. Does the place cause this to happen or does your very old age as measured in the real world cause your bodies to disintegrate this way? I don't know and I expect you don't either. I'm not sure it makes any difference. Any way we don't have time to debate the question. We still must find the magic keys and take them out of this place. I expect Elizabeth will come after us in here as soon as she can take back her wand. We need to complete our mission before she does that." Carly said.

"I agree. Last time I came down here, I reached the keys but Elizabeth prevented me from taking them. She threatened to kill me. I backed down and left. I have often thought about what would have happened if I had brought the keys to the surface. This time I'm going to find out. Now follow me, the keys are on a pedestal in the center of the cavern." Oh and someone pick up the spear. We may need it." Beatrice said.

After Terrance picked up the spear, the quest team walked slowly and cautiously down the path. Cynthia had a question for Beatrice.

"Beatrice are there any other traps or creatures we have to face?"

"Yes the scariest part comes now. Elizabeth put some kind of memory spell in this area right at the beginning of the main cavern, where she placed the keys. Think of the worst experience you ever had. The spell makes you relive it. The funny part is it only affects some of the people walking though this area on the way down but no one as far as I know on the way up. If someone starts experiencing this spell, all of us have to prevent this person from wandering back to the traps behind us. Barbara already showed us what happens then."

Skylar heard Beatrice explain the memory spell but seconds later walked with her friend Bonnie on a dark road in a moonless night. The crickets created a constant hum in the background. The night felt warm and a little sticky. Skylar could hear each step she and her friend took. Eight again, she noticed how different she felt in her small body. Bonnie and her decided to walk to Bonnie's home which lay a mile from the birthday they just attended rather than wait for Bonnie's mother who had been delayed. They didn't tell the adults at the party where they went. The night seemed to grow darker. Fear suddenly grabbed Skylar who spoke nervously to her friend.

"Bonnie, I don't think this was a very good idea, but we're kind of stuck half way between the two houses. I guess we have to keep going."

"Yeah, I should have told you, some man kidnapped a little girl near here two weeks ago. I didn't think about it until just now. Maybe we need to walk faster." Bonnie said.

"If we walk any faster I think we will have to run but maybe that's not a bad idea. I can swear that I just heard the bushes move behind us? Except for the locusts, it's so quiet the noise really stands out."

"Yeah I heard it. Run." Bonnie screamed.

As Bonnie yelled, a man emerged from the bushes and started moving toward the girls. The girls ran as fast as they could away from him, but with each step, the faster man drew closer. Skylar could feel her heart beating in her chest and the sweat running down her cheeks. The man could almost reach the girls now. Skylar smelled his bad breath. He spoke.

"Now where are you pretty little girls headed? Why don't you come visit my house?"

Just as the man reached for the girls, a car skidded around the corner and bore down on the man. The headlights caused the man to shield his eyes. He hesitated a moment, allowing the girls to escape his grasp. The car screeched to a halt. Bonnie's mother leaped out of the car and trained her 9mm Beretta on the man. She screamed.

"I'M A POLICE DETECTIVE. GET AWAY FROM MY DAUGHTER OR I'LL BLOW YOUR BRAINS OUT. ON THE GROUND NOW!"

The man recognizing the rage of a protective mother quietly lowered himself to his knees and put his hands behind his neck. Skylar woke up. Her whole body shook. Samantha and Cynthia stood in front of Skylar preventing her from entering the trap area. The panicked running Skylar in her dreams would have triggered one of the traps in this magic world cave.

Meanwhile, ten-year old Carly sat on a mule behind her parents on a trail down the Grand Canyon. Her butt hurt and she tried to look straight ahead rather than down the three thousand foot cliff a short distance to her left. The intense heat and dryness of the canyon made her throat raw with thirst. She coughed a little from the dust the wind sometimes blew in her face. Carly wanted to appear brave to her father but she felt icy fear move up her legs, which had begun to shake. Carly kept telling herself that it would be all right, that these mules took tourists like her to the bottom of the canyon every day. Then she heard a rattle and saw a rattlesnake suddenly move in front of her mule. The calm mule suddenly went wild bucking Carly off. She fell on the trail and began rolling to the edge.

Carly desperately tried to stop but the ground felt loose and she couldn't gain a good hand or foothold on anything. Out of the corner of her eye, she saw the trail guide take a long staff and sweep the rattlesnake off the edge of the cliff. As Carly's legs slid off the edge of the cliff, she reached for the guide's hand. At the last possible moment, he grabbed her hand and pulled her to safety. Carly's entire body trembled with fear. Seconds later, her mother hugged her. She could feel her mother's tears drip on her upturned face.

Carly woke up in the arms of Beatrice and Skylar. Her body shook just as it did in her dream. She managed to mutter a quiet thanks. A lever for one of the traps lay a few centimeters away from her left foot. Carly wondered why both she and Skylar moved toward the hidden levers in their dreams. Elizabeth had to have something to do with it.

Beatrice spoke. "Okay we're through the dream area. Looks like only two of you had the dreams. Even though you look shook up, you managed to avoid injury. I had the dream the first time I came here but luckily not this time. The last time I received a bad bruise while in my dream when I hit the wall. Now that we're in the cavern, the keys are only fifteen meters away in the center of the cavern. Let's walk there carefully in a single line. I don't remember any more levers on the cavern floor but you can't be too careful in this place."

A few minutes later, the quest team reached the pedestal and looked upon the twenty-six keys sitting there. Samantha began to put her hand out to take a key but Beatrice stopped her.

"I've thought about this for a long time. What if the pedestal stands on a lever like the ones at the entrance to the cave? Maybe when the keys are removed the lever is triggered. Then we all end up like Barbara with a spear or arrow in our chest. So before we remove any of the keys we need to find twenty-six stones of about the same weight as the keys and replace each key we take with a rock. If we do it correctly, the pedestal will have the same weight when we finish that it has now. The lever if it is there won't be triggered. What do you think?"

"Beatrice I think that's a great idea. You can never be too cautious. Elizabeth wouldn't have made it this easy for us to take the keys. She certainly hasn't made it easy so far." Skylar said.

Without further discussion, the quest team explored the cavern looking for small rocks. After fifteen minutes, they collected a large pile of rocks. Beatrice and Carly selected twenty-six rocks from the pile of the same approximate size. When they had them separated, Beatrice and Carly turned to the rest of the group. Beatrice spoke.

"Everyone's life is at stake here. We've selected twenty-six rocks one for each key. If anyone wants to exchange one rock for another, please say so."

Terrance walked to the rock pile and removed one rock larger than the others. Terrance replaced it with another rock from the main pile. He said simply.

"I think this rock is better."

"Agreed-alright this is how we are going to do this. I'll remove a key and put a rock in its place at the same moment. I'll hand the key back to one of you and then make the next switch until all the keys are removed from the pedestal. The rest of you lie on the ground in case this doesn't work. If anyone else wants this task, please raise your hand." Beatrice said.

"No, I think we are all happy that you're taking the responsibility." Cynthia replied.

The operation went very smoothly. In a matter of minutes, each of the team had several of the keys in their pockets and the pedestal now had rocks where the keys had been.

"We did it! Now all we have to do is to retrace our steps and rejoin the others. Let's go." Carly said happily. All the quest team rose to their feet and congratulated each other. At just this moment, however, the quest team heard a loud roar. They turned toward the noise and saw a very large white tiger emerging from a door in the east wall. Something they had done caused the door to open. The crouching tiger walked quietly on its paws toward the middle of the cavern, its eyes focused on the quest team. While the rest of the quest team hesitated, Cynthia quietly moved back to the pedestal. She spoke to her comrades.

"Lie down on the ground again. I'll sweep the rocks off the pedestal and fall to the ground along with you. If the pedestal is on a lever, we might have a chance against this beast. I don't want to think about what will happen if the pedestal is not on a lever. I'll wait to the tiger comes close before I sweep the rocks off."

"I have the spear. I'll fight the tiger if this doesn't work." Terrance said lying on the ground.

"Thank you Terrance. I hope it doesn't come to that." Samantha said.

As soon as the quest team lay down, the tiger broke into a run, quickly making up the distance between them. Cynthia swept the rocks off the pedestal and fell to the ground as she did so. At first nothing happened; then the pedestal began to move upward. The tiger leaped for the closest kid, Skylar, but at the same moment, arrows and spears burst out of the walls of the cavern. Four spears and five arrows pierced the tiger. Skylar rolled out of the way as the heavy tiger collapsed onto the space where Skylar just lay. The tiger moved a little then fell silent. Seconds later the tiger glowed then turned into dust and ash. Skylar shaking with fear slowly stood and spoke. The tiger fell only a few centimeters from her.

"I've never been so scared in my whole life! Elizabeth certainly had some surprises waiting for us. All I know is that I've had enough of this place. Let's get out of here!"

"Follow me. I led you into the cave and now I'll lead you out. Oh and as before, each of you should pick up several spears. There must be at least twelve of them on the ground. We may need them to fight the bats or whatever other creatures Elizabeth sends after us." Beatrice said.

Each of the quest team picked up two spears and followed Beatrice in a single file up the cave path. At first, the journey back went well. Unlike the way down, the quest team remained largely silent and focused on any potential threats. As Beatrice said, no one had a bad dream as they went back through this area at the end of the cavern. Some time later, just before they reached the bat nesting area, Cynthia spoke.

"Even though we have some bat guano still on us, I think we ought put some more on our bodies. It seemed to help last time. None of us received any bites. If they come after us again, Constance, Calico and Barbara can scream as Constance and Calico did last time."

"Yeah and this time if these measures fail, we can form a tight circle and stab the bats as they attack with the spears we picked up. If we kill enough of them maybe they'll stop attacking." Carly added.

"A good idea Carly--alright, after we smear ourselves with more guano, we'll walk as quietly as possible underneath the creatures and just hope they don't wake up again." Beatrice said.

As the quest team walked underneath the bats, they noticed that they moved less than the last time. Apparently their recent flight tired them a little. To their surprise they made it past this nesting area without an attack. Now they only had to avoid the dangerous hole and they would be out of the cave. As they relaxed a little, the quest team heard a loud commotion. Elizabeth and Rachel fought just ahead on the path. They threw powerful bolts of energy at each other. The air sizzled. Elizabeth had regained her wand. Elizabeth hurled a bolt at Rachel that drove her over the hole, but instead of dropping into the hole, Rachel floated past it. Rachel fought back with a powerful energy surge of her own driving Elizabeth into the wall.

Skylar spoke nervously.

"The witches will wake up the bats with all that noise and energy. Then we'll be trapped between them and the bats. What can we do?"

"We'll follow the plan. Constance, Calico and I will float over there and start screaming the moment the bats attack. The rest of you will form a circle and stab any of the nasty creatures that come after you." Barbara said.

Just as they assumed their positions, they heard Elizabeth yell.

"Awake my bats. Kill all the children underneath you. Their blood will taste sweet and delicious."

The bats, as if they understood Elizabeth's command, suddenly flew off the ceiling toward them. Unlike last time, their bat guano only slowed the bat's attack. The bats seemed to smell them despite the guano. Constance and Barbara began to scream. Some of the bats flew toward them shrieking, but the rest attacked the quest team. The quest team reacted by stabbing any bat that came after them with a spear in each hand. As with the tiger, the bats glowed and turned into dust when they died. Unlike last time, the quest team couldn't avoid some bites. While they protected their faces and necks, the bats bit them on their arms and legs. Carly and Skylar uttered curses, but the rest of the group avoided saying such things preferring to exclaim words such as ouch.

Meanwhile, Rachel and Elizabeth spoke loudly to each other as they fought. Rachel said.

"Elizabeth, you're all alone in fighting to keep us here. Everyone has turned against you."

"Why should I care? I put a sleeping spell on the girls at the cave entrance. The quest team is busy fighting hundreds of bats. It's just you and me and I have always been stronger than you." Elizabeth responded.

"Not quite—if you look behind, you'll see the girls you put to sleep advancing on you. I neutralized your sleep spell and I'll keep neutralizing your spells until they reach you." Rachel challenged.

"This is our chance. We'll never be able to kill all of these bats. We have to go after the person causing all this—Elizabeth. We'll move toward her in a formation just like soldiers do in a battle." Terrance said.

The tightly packed quest team nodded their heads and began moving toward Elizabeth. Within minutes, they approached Elizabeth who focused all her attention on fighting Rachel. Constance, who hovered off the ground, spoke.

"The rest of the girls we left at the cave entrance are approaching Elizabeth from the other direction. Throw your extra spears to them and you can attack Elizabeth from both directions."

Beatrice yelled to the other girls coming down the path from the entrance. "Take these six spears and attack Elizabeth from your side. We'll attack her from this side."

With that comment, the quest team threw the extra spears handle first toward their friends on the other side of Elizabeth. The girls from the entrance picked them up and ran at Elizabeth. The quest team abandoned their tight circle and ran from their side, ignoring the bats as best they could. Elizabeth seeing the pincer movement closing on her turned toward the quest team with rage in her eyes. She raised her hands above her heard and sent balls of energy toward the girls yelling as she did so.

"Take that!"

The fire from Elizabeth's hands knocked out most of the quest team, but Skylar and Carly ducked under the fire and kept coming. Elizabeth raised her hands again but whirled at the last second to see the other girls rushing at her from the rear. She threw another bolt of energy from her hands knocking all but two of the girls on the other side to the ground. She said.

"There I have knocked out most of you pesky girls. You can never defeat me."

Skylar and Carly, however, ran even faster, managing to thrust their spears into Elizabeth's legs as she turned toward them. Before she could strike Carly and Skylar at point blank range, the two girls from the other side also thrust their spears into Elizabeth's legs.

Elizabeth screamed in agony saying, "I'll kill you for that!"

Yet, Elizabeth before carrying out her threat needed to avoid further injury. She waved her wand and began to rise out of the girls' striking distance but did so too late. Without any bat guano on her, Elizabeth's bleeding legs attracted a large number of thirsty vampire bats. One attacked her leg followed by another and another. Elizabeth yelled and struck several of the bats on her legs with a bolt of energy from her wand, sending them writhing to the ground. As she did so, Elizabeth scolded the remaining bats.

"Stop attacking me. I 'm your creator. I'll kill you all if I have to."

The bats, however, ignored her. They kept attacking. Elizabeth screaming even louder continued to send one bolt of energy after another at her own legs knocking vampire bat after vampire bat to the ground, but more bats covered her than she knocked out. The bolts of energy also burned Elizabeth's legs, causing her to cry out in pain. When the bats completely covered Elizabeth and prevented her from using her wand, Elizabeth swatted the bats with her arms, but this proved to be even less effective than her bolts of energy. As soon as Elizabeth swatted one away another would take its place. The terrible chaos continued for several minutes Elizabeth screaming and knocking the bats with her arms and the bats flapping and biting. Then slowly Elizabeth as those that died before her began to glow. Moments later, Elizabeth's body turned to ash and dust, falling slowly to the ground in a shower. With no blood left to drink and their creator dead, the bats calmed. As if someone gave them a new order they flew back to their perches on the ceiling, folded their wings and fell asleep. The girls knocked to the ground by Elizabeth slowly regained their feet, shaking their arms and heads as they did so.

Then quite suddenly everyone looked up toward a bright apparition high in the air and heard Elizabeth's voice as she took form next to Constance, Calico and Barbara.

"You think you have defeated me, but you're wrong. Without my magic, this place will begin to dissolve. All of you except Carly and Skylar if they get out of here in time will be trapped in my world and die unless the keys are used to open the locks. You'll never reach the locks in time. You'll become dust and ash like me and never live the life I took from you."

"They may die that's true, but everyone here will go into the light and the beautiful world there. You, however, will go into the dark red light where there is only torment and pain. I've seen spirits go in there before. It's not a pretty sight." Constance said angrily pointing a ghostly finger at Elizabeth.

Elizabeth looked shocked. She began to say something then stopped. A moment later she disappeared.

"Hurry, give us all the keys. Carly and I will do everything we can to reach the locks in time. You have our word on that." Skylar said.

The rest of the quest team hurriedly turned over the keys to Skylar and Carly who put them in their pockets. As soon as they secured the keys, they ran for the cave entrance careful to stay close to the wall and away from the hidden hole. The rest of the children in the World in Between ran along next to them encouraging Skylar and Carly to run as fast as they could.

Back to the Real World

As Carly and Skylar ran, the World in Between changed. The vibrant colors began to dull to more normal colors and the dream like quality of the place became more real. The children of this world began to glow very faintly. Everyone knew what that meant. When the large group of children reached the doorway, Rachel suddenly appeared.

"I'm using all my power to keep this place from disappearing but I don't' know how long I can keep it going. Elizabeth created this place not me. Hurry, try the door--it should open easily as Elizabeth's spell should have died with her. Wait a minute—the door has been destroyed from the outside. There are people out there. They must not come in here. They could die with us if the World in Between disappears."

Before leaving, Carly spoke.

"Rachel, I'll keep those people out if I can. They'll probably follow Skylar and I when we leave. Maybe everyone can just walk out of here like us. This world is crumbling after all."

"No I'm afraid they can't, I can't. You heard Elizabeth. The spell will keep us here until we disappear along with this world. The walls of this world will prevent us from leaving. Now hurry and unlock our locks. That is the only way we can escape." Rachel responded.

"We will on behalf of all of you. You can count on us." Skylar replied.

Carly and Skylar ran through the barriers with little trouble waving goodbye to Rachel and the inhabitants of the World in Between. They didn't know whether the keys allowed them to exit the World in Between or whether the death of Elizabeth did so. To their surprise, they saw a large number of workers cutting holes on both sides of the World in Between entrance. The shocked workers didn't say anything at first as the girls ran past them and surprisingly turned left out of the corridor as opposed to the way they first came into the place. The startled workers didn't have a clear sight of the running girls as the debris blocking the corridor had only been partially cleared. Then the foreman realizing what just happened called to the girls.

"Are you Skylar and Carly? We're digging here to free you and here you are. They're a lot of people who want to talk to you, including the headmistress of Tanglewood, your parents, and the police department to name a few. You had a lot of people worried."

"Yes, I'm Carly and this is Skylar. We're fine. We'll be glad to talk with anyone who wants to speak with us, but first we have something very important to do. We need to save the lives of some young girls. We have very little time to do what we need to do." Carly yelled without slowing down or turning around.

"I don't know whether I can let you go. You'll have to come with me. If there are young girls at risk, we can help." The supervisor yelled back at the disappearing girls.

The girls ignored the supervisor whose voice began to fade in the distance. They never slowed after running through the barrier. Skylar whispered through her labored breaths.

"I sure hope there are stairs to the outside in this part of the tunnel. They should be here as we didn't see them in the other part of the tunnel or the corridor, but even if we find them we might not be able to use them."

"We have no choice. Running back the other way, the adults would have at least held onto us if not locked us in a room. The children of the World in Between and Rachel would have died while we tried to convince those adults to let us unlock the locks."

"You're right but this outside entrance better appear soon. I can hear boots in the tunnel. It sounds like someone may be headed this way."

"They probably split up, half coming our way half the other. As adults they will be faster than us. Wait! I see a break in the wall up ahead on the left. Cross your fingers that this is what we are looking for. If it is, we must try and hide. We could never climb some ancient stairs without our chasers finding us."

The girls turned down the corridor as soon as they reached it. They went only a few yards before they found the very old steps to the outside. Fortunately, the steps had some space behind them, which couldn't be seen very well from the front. The girls quickly hid behind the steps and turned off their flashlight and lantern. They both controlled their breathing as best they could. They heard spiders and rats crawling around in the space but they bravely ignored the sounds.

Two men with flashlights appeared only a minute later. They shone their lights down the short corridor but saw nothing. They walked to the stairs and looked up seeing that the door above hadn't been opened in a very long time. Cobwebs hung from the door to the walls. The tallest man who the girls recognized as the supervisor said.

"They didn't come down this corridor. I'm not even sure they came this way down the tunnel. We thought we saw a light ahead but it could have been a reflection from our lights. Still, we should take this tunnel to its end. It supposedly connects with the Worthington house. They could come out of the tunnel there."

"I agree boss. We're wasting time here. Let's go."

The girls heard the workers heavy boots leave the corridor and head down the tunnel. They waited two precious minutes until they could no longer hear the footsteps before coming out of their hiding place. After knocking the spiders off each other and pulling off their sticky webs, the pair climbed the stairs until they reached the trap door at the top. The partially rotten stairs creaked and groaned. Skylar nervously said.

"We better get out of here before these stairs collapse and we end up with broken legs. I'm trying not to think how many times those spiders bit me."

"I am at the trap door to the outside. I'm pushing on it but it isn't budging.

Climb up next to me. We both have to push on it. There is probably some soil or other stuff on top of it." Carly answered.

Using all their strength, the two girls pushed the old rusty door up a few inches. Skylar almost fell off the stairs, but Carly grabbed her. Carly spoke again.

"Come on Skylar we have to push harder we almost have it."

With a mighty shove from both girls, the door creaked open all the way, leaves, twigs and dirt falling away from it. The girls quickly climbed out of the tunnel as the stairs collapsed behind them. They brushed the debris that had fallen from their hair and stood for a moment in the woods.

"Whew that was close. We almost ended up with those broken legs. Okay, let's imagine the tunnel underground and follow it back to the school. I think we're in the woods, east of the front gate, just where we need to be. There probably was a path long ago but it's almost certainly overgrown now."

"The girls followed the tunnel in their minds as best they could. Carly still had her backpack. Skylar lost hers in the cave. Carly always kept a compass in her backpack for emergencies and used this compass to adjust their position a few times. They wanted to go northwest toward the school. Without it, they would have certainly become lost. The way proved to be difficult. The leaves hid rocks, holes and parts of trees. Skylar twisted her ankle a little but didn't sprain it. The girls also encountered bramble bushes and vines that they had to push out of their way. They each received a number of scratches to add to their spider bites. Skylar couldn't help but express some frustration.

"We're taking too long. The World in Between kids and Rachel may already be dead. We might be lost and in trouble ourselves. My left ankle already hurts. Even if we reach the front gate, there may be people there preventing us from climbing it and opening the locks."

"Skylar we can only do our best. We will never forgive ourselves if we don't. Remember those kids in that world were prevented from living their lives. We have to try to give them some of that time back."

Skylar slowly nodded her head then put her hand up.

"Wait—listen carefully. I think that is a car straight ahead. We may have reached the road to the school."

The girls ran faster and in a few minutes suddenly burst out of the woods onto the Tanlgewood road. The car they heard had just passed through the gate. The gate closed as the girls ran toward it.

When Skylar and Carly reached the gate, no one could be seen. A camera pointed at them, but the guards in the school only looked at the camera pictures when someone pressed the button and asked for the gate to be opened. In the old days, a Tanglewood employee stood guard at the gate but after budget cuts the school went to this new system. Without hesitating, Carly climbed the swirling iron of the front gate and found a place where she could reach the locks underneath the iron bars covering them. She called down to Skylar.

"Hold my legs. I don't want to fall. I'll try a key from my pocket on the locks until I find the right one. Then I'll move onto the next key and lock. When I have used all my keys, you can hand your keys up to me."

Carly tried fourteen locks before she found the one that the first key fit. She quickly turned the key and the lock opened. She had even worse luck with the second key. She tried sixteen locks before she found the correct key. After she unlocked this lock, however, her luck improved. She unlocked the third lock on the tenth try. After opening ten locks, Carly started to complain.

"My feet hurt, my back hurts, and the bars over the locks are rubbing my hands raw. We have fifteen more locks to open. Do you want to try?"

"I would but I hurt my ankle in the forest. Any way you are a much better climber than me. Believe me, holding onto your legs isn't any fun either. My ankle is killing me and my back hurts too." Skylar replied.

"Alright I have three keys left. When I finish opening these locks hand the others up to me. No matter how uncomfortable this is lives are at stake here."

After Carly opened the thirteenth lock, Skylar began to hand over the remainder of the keys. Since most of the locks had been opened, Carly now found the correct lock in only three or four tries. After Carly unlocked the fifteenth lock, the speaker next to the gate came to life.

"This is the headmistress. Stop what you are doing at once! A guard is on his way to your location at this very moment to arrest you. The construction foreman told me you ran past him and talked about saving some young girls. I knew you headed for the gate and the keys. You have to stop acting out this silly fantasy of yours."

"For what? We're saving lives here by opening the locks that kept in place curses on the girls who were once students at this school. We met these kids when we journeyed to the World In Between. Their world is collapsing after the death of Elizabeth the witch who started this whole thing. If this world collapses, anyone still in it will die. Already several have been released. If you go to the corridor entrance to this strange world you should see some of these kids that is of course if we released them in time. Meanwhile, we'll keep releasing kids until you stop us. Any way, even if everything I'm saying is pure fantasy as you claim, what harm are we doing opening these old locks? No one has found these keys in over two hundred years. They have one purpose: to open these locks. So that is what we are doing." Skylar responded.

"You have no right to the keys. They're the property of the school." The headmistress said.

"We've no intention of keeping them. We'll give you the keys after we open them. They are yours or the school's or whoever's. Believe me--my back and ankle is killing me holding up Carly as I am. Carly is hurting even more opening those locks and holding onto that fence up there. We'll climb down the fence as soon as we finish." Skylar said.

While Skylar talked, Carly continued to open locks. She already unlocked lock number eighteen. Carly, however, noticed the school security car coming toward them at high speed. Carly only had a few more minutes. She tired to go even faster. Her hands bled from moving so quickly. As Carly unlocked the nineteenth lock, Elizabeth suddenly appeared to her. She spoke with anger and authority.

"Stop what you're doing or I'll throw you off of here and break your neck. You're ruining my curse."

"Skylar, Elizabeth just showed up. She says if I don't stop she is going to break my neck."

"Don't listen to her. She is just a ghost. Keep opening those locks!" Skylar replied.

Carly opened the twentieth lock, but felt a strong tug from Elizabeth who tried to pull her off the fence. Carly held on as hard as she could but felt her grip slipping on the fence. Just then, Barbara, Calico and Constance appeared. Calico said.

"Get away from them Elizabeth. Your time terrorizing these girls is over."

"Never. I will keep these girls in my world forever." Elizabeth responded.

Elizabeth raised her hands to throw her fire spell at Barbara, Calico and Constance, but only a small flame came from her fingers. Constance laughed.

"As a ghost you don't have that kind of power anymore."

"That isn't my only spell. You'll regret those words." Elizabeth snarled.

Elizabeth raised her hands again for another spell but before she could say the magic words, Carly and Barbara grabbed Elizabeth and Calico jumped into her face. With three of them against one, Elizabeth relaxed her grip on Carly allowing Barbara and Constance to tear Carly from Elizabeth's grip. Free again, Carly quickly regained her grip on the fence and her balance. Constance smiled at Elizabeth as she slipped out of their grip. Elizabeth backed up several feet and turned toward Constance and Barbara with fury on her face. She lashed out at them.

"I'll destroy you for interfering with me."

"No you won't. You can't. You've foolishly used up your energy fighting with us and trying to issue a fire spell. See that black and red mass whirling in back of you. If you'd preserved your energy you might have been able to resist it but now you can't. See how you're moving toward it. Nothing can save you now. Your headed to a very bad place." Constance said.

"No. I won't go there. Even as a ghost I have things I must do." Elizabeth said as she began to descend into the swirling mass.

"Goodbye Elizabeth. Your curse has ended." Barbara said.

"No please help me! I don't want to fall into that black hole." Elizabeth pleaded.

"You're beyond help Elizabeth." Constance said.

"Yes, you are finally paying for all the mean things you did to the Key Girls and Boy, and even me." Calico added.

Seconds later, Elizabeth entered the red and black swirling mass, screaming as she disappeared.

"Carly and Skylar, Barbara, Calico and I need to rest. We used up a lot of energy fighting Elizabeth. We'll come back to you as soon as we have our energy back." Constance said through Carly.

Carly nodded at Barbara, Calico and Constance and said.

"Thank you for saving me and the remaining Key Girls and Boy, a good name you just invented for all our new friends. You will always be my ghost friends and my heroes. Skylar thanks to our ghost friends, Elizabeth has gone to Hades the Dark World. She'll never bother us again!"

"Yeah, thank you so much for finally sending that evil witch to where she belonged. I couldn't help Carly fight Elizabeth and still support her on the fence. I almost lost my balance. As Carly said, you saved us. I couldn't see what happened but I knew you were there helping us." Skylar said.

After smiling at their friends, Constance, Calico and Barbara disappeared. Meanwhile, Carly resumed her task and unlocked the twenty first lock. Carly found the twenty second lock and managed to unlock it but became a little distracted when the Tanglewood Security Guard brought his car to a stop in front of the gate and yelled at her.

"Stop what you're doing and come down here right now! Don't make me come up there."

Carly, trying to ignore the angry guard, replied as she unlocked the twenty third lock.

"I have three more locks to unlock. I'll come down as soon as I unlock them. This key here fits the twenty-fourth. There it's done. Now I have two keys and two locks remaining. Oh this one fits the 25th. The lock is open. That was an easy one. Now, I'm fitting the final key into its lock. Hey where did you go Skylar? I'm hanging on for dear life?"

"The guard pulled me off the fence, hurry" Skylar said.

"I'm on the final lock the 26th. It's sticking a little but here it goes. There it is; I'm done with the twenty-sixth and final lock. I have to say, unlocking the locks with both hands was pretty neat, even if the old bars scratched my hands pretty badly. I may have to have a tetanus shot. Guard whatever your name is you can take your lousy hand off my foot now. I hope your not some kind of pervert."

When the guard let go, Carly landed on the ground. She glared at the security guard.

"Hey you could of hurt me pulling on my foot like that."

The security officer didn't answer. Instead, he put Carly and Skylar in handcuffs. Skylar angrily addressed the guard.

"What are you arresting us for?"

"Damage to property and trespassing,"

"What is this the Gestapo? My family started this school. The school still sits on my family property. It is leased to the school for 99-year intervals. I can't trespass on my own property. Anyway, we are both students at this school and belong here. As to damage, there is no damage. The locks still work. In fact, we have returned lost property, the keys to the school." Skylar said.

"I have my orders and I'm going to carry them out." The guard replied.

As the guard led Carly and Skylar away, both dreamed of having a nice long shower to wash off the bat guano. With their task completed, the girls began to focus on the guano's terrible smell. They smiled a little thinking that the guard's car might pick up some of the smell and then the silent and angry guard would have to smell the guano just like them.

A Moment of Freedom

Samantha marched out of the World in Between into a corridor. No one appeared to be in the corridor but all sorts of strange looking machines Samantha did not recognize stood there. The workers had run off to chase Carly and Skylar. The rest of the people trapped in the World In Between started to appear next to Samantha. Soon the entire in between world population except Elizabeth stood in a group. Rachel, who appeared last, addressed them all.

"It looks like we are back in reality as live people. I know this corridor and the tunnel connected to it. The duke showed me the tunnel before I confronted Elizabeth. I will lead us back to Tanglewood that is of course if these curious lights dangling from wires above us go all the way back there. Some of them seem to work while others don't. We have no candles or lanterns. Everyone we ever knew is dead in this time. We may not even have any living descendants. More than two hundred years is a very long time. I don't how people will react to us. Some may be threatened. Others won't believe us. Still others may try to study us. For our part, this world may be very strange. From the few hints we had from Carly and Skylar technology has become very advanced. Imagine looking into a piece of glass and seeing an event or a play about an event. It will be like magic to us. For the time being, I think we should only speak to the outside world through Carly and Skylar. They've been to our World in Between and saved us from Elizabeth. They will understand us and have our best interests at heart."

"I agree. We have to be careful. Just before our time, they burned people for things happening they couldn't explain. Hopefully, this world is more advanced than that but times change people don't." Samantha said.

"I agree with you Samantha. All right, let's go and find out about this new world. I don't know how much time we have here. I'm 269 years old. I doubt I'm fourteen anymore, even if I look like it." Beatrice said.

"I think I can help with this. I'm of this time and lived in the World in Between. I can support your story. Also, I can help everyone get out of here. I'm from this time." Tiffany said.

"Thanks Tiffany that will be helpful." Rachel said.

Tiffany led the way out the corridor and to the right along the duke's tunnel. Everyone else followed in mostly a single file line. More of the curious glass bulbs lighted the way. The World in Between group wondered why these small bulbs gave off light like the sun. They resembled the lights Carly and Skylar had but unlike hers they had no battery attached. The lights continued through a door into a larger tunnel. The Key Girls and Terrance continued to follow the lights. When the lights ended at a door, Tiffany opened the door and the rest followed. The basement behind the door puzzled all of them except Tiffany. Some of the walls looked a little like Prudence's house but the machinery, lights, wires and pipes didn't look at all familiar. They found stairs in a place they remembered stairs were long ago, and walked up to the first floor of the school. They passed some workers on the way looking for Carly and Skylar, who only stared at them. When the large group reached the first floor, what they saw seemed a little familiar and yet very different. The school had grown tremendously from its beginnings as Prudence's house.

Meanwhile, Carly and Skylar sat in the headmistress' office. The guard removed the handcuffs but the headmistress still appeared to be quite angry.

"You girls went missing for three days! Your parents were sick with worry. The police looked everywhere. We even hired contractors to dig around the weird place your friends said you hid and to gain entry from the side. Then you just walk out of that weird place like nothing happened and open the locks, which have been a symbol at this school for over two hundred years. And my god what is that terrible smell? You girls need a bath."

"Actually, all four of us Skylar, Jade, Peggy and I walked up to the World In Between door. The evil witch Elizabeth drew Skylar and I inside but wouldn't let Peggy and Jade in. Peggy and Jade must have told you this. We merely worked as hard as we could to help the people inside this weird world to escape back to this world. We did what every girl that has attended this school for over two hundred years wanted to do, we found the keys to the magic locks, unlocked them and forever destroyed the curse Elizabeth put on this place. At to the smell, we smeared bat guano all over us to help prevent the Vampire Bats from attacking us." Carly said.

"Yeah, we gave all those kids and one boy the chance to live again. We don't know if they actually got out or not because the World in Between was collapsing as we escaped from it. If any of them did make it out, they should have come out the entrance you were excavating as we did. Has anyone looked for them?" Skylar asked.

"You forgot to mention the two boys that accompanied you. Anyway, this whole thing is crazy. Witches, spells, shimmering barriers, and magical worlds don't exist, can't exist. Also people don't live to be two hundred fifty years old. So of course no one has looked for these children of long ago. I'd advise you to stop talking about it. Otherwise, someone is going to lock you up in a mental institution." Tabatha said.

"Okay then how do you explain the shimmering wall and the world everyone saw beyond it? You must have seen it. You had workmen down there." Carly said.

"I didn't' see it and neither did you. You just thought you saw it." Tabatha said. Just then, her secretary came running into the office, her eyes wide.

"Headmistress I think we have another crisis. I saw it myself when I went for coffee. Twenty some kids and an adult just walked into the main hall in costumes that look like they came out of the revolutionary war. They are just walking around the school staring and asking questions. Some of them smell awful just like the girls you have sitting here. The adult is asking for Carly and Skylar, their saviors. Almost all the kids are complaining about being hungry. They say they haven't eaten in a very long time. Oh and by the way, Tiffany is with them. I'll call her parents immediately. "

"That's Rachel the good witch asking for us. Tell her we will be right with her. I'm so happy they made it out of the World in Between in one piece. We're going to have to come up with a plan for dealing with these people. With all they went through, they need to enjoy as much of their life they have left as possible." Skylar said.

"Yeah, we need to give them an identity and all the papers that go with having one. We need to figure out what role they will play in this modern world. There is just so much to do." Carly added.

"This can't possibly be happening, but if it is I don't see how it's my responsibility. I can't take care of all these people with the exception of Tiffany of course. They need places to sleep and food to eat." Tabatha said with shock registering on her face.

"Headmistress, I don't need to remind you that with the exception of the boy and Rachel, all of these girls were and are Tanglewood students. They're your responsibility. I know my father would be very upset if you didn't treat the duke's daughter Samantha well. I think several of the other girls also have living relatives still involved in the school. I'm sure they would feel the same way." Skylar said.

"You have a point there but I'll still need to convene the School Board of Directors and ask them what to do. Meanwhile, let's take them to the cafeteria and feed them. The last girls should be finishing up their lunches about now. We can at least see who is there and compare them to the girls who went missing in the later 1700's. I think we have a list of the missing girls in the archives. Oh and Penny, find the group wandering around our halls and bring them to the cafeteria. Then go and get Jade and Peggy. I think they should be there too. As to Tiffany, she needs to come to my office so she can speak with her parents. She can join the other girls later if she wants to do so." Tabatha said as she began to organize herself for the strange meeting that lay ahead.

Skylar and Carly followed the headmistress out of her office. Peggy and Jade joined them outside Tabatha's office. As a group they soon encountered, Rachel, the Key Girls and Boy in the main hall. Tabatha after greeting the large group with a simple "hello and follow me," led them into the dinning room. Tabatha then sat all of them at a long table. While the group seated themselves, Tabatha waved at the cook who had come out of the kitchen to supervise the clean up. The chef came running up to the table. After a short conversation with the headmistress, the cook hurried back into the kitchen. The headmistress finally spoke at length.

"I'm Tabatha the headmistress of Tanglewood. I'm having a very hard time believing all of this. It's not every day I sit down with two hundred fifty year old people who look like children if that is who you are. I've ordered some food for all of you. The main dish is spaghetti and meatballs. There is also salad, fruit, milk, juice, coffee and tea. You may not be familiar with the spaghetti dish but I think you will like it. I have a list of all the missing children from those terrible years of the curse. Write your name down on one of the blank sheets of paper and I will compare your name to the names on the sheet. Also, indicate whether you had a portrait painted of you. I think the school had one painted for each class before photographs became available, but I have no way of knowing whether you sat for one of these or not. I think I have seen some of these group portraits in the archives. Anything we can do to verify that you are who you say you are will be very helpful to us. I'm not even sure what I should be saying to you. Skylar and Carly swear that you are the missing children from the curse but I don't know how to accept something that seems impossible."

"I'm Rachel, the witch who battled the evil Elizabeth. She cast the magic key spell. I just reached my twenty third birthday and accepted a marriage proposal from a nice young man when the duke approached me about using witchcraft to fight Elizabeth. My mother practiced witchcraft and I joined her coven at an early age. I studied the discipline very hard and had gained a solid reputation as a good witch by the time the duke approached me. Despite my teachings and beliefs, I developed a healthy skepticism of my craft. In all the years I practiced, I could not attribute one result solely to the casting of a spell. Rather, the result could also be explained by natural means. Nonetheless the duke offered me a sum of money a woman to be married could not refuse. So, I took all my witchcraft equipment and came to this school for the contest.

"When I challenged Elizabeth, I confronted powers that I still after all these years have a hard time explaining or believing. Elizabeth evoked these powers and controlled them. From the very first moment, I served as a mere toy of Elizabeth. She threw me around like a doll and twisted my limbs in knots. While in this deplorable state, I remembered an ancient and powerful spell I learned that made the spell giver the victim of their spell along with the intended victim. I cast this spell on Elizabeth as best I could and waited. After Elizabeth grew tired of torturing me, she cast me into her world, but because of my spell, she entered the World In Between with me. I couldn't believe then and still can't believe now that it worked, but after Elizabeth and I entered the World in Between, no one else came. The part of the spell that caused girls at Halloween to be taken into the World in Between seemed to have been broken. At the same time, none of us could find a way out of the World in Between not even Elizabeth. The spells she cast would not release her no matter what counter spells she tried. I think that is one of the reasons she is so mean. She left a husband and two children behind in Australia that she never saw again. We have remained in this world until Carly and Skylar came for us. Oh and over the years, my magic improved. I don't know if the World In Between magic caused it to do so or my skill grew, but I could at least prevent Elizabeth from doing her worst to the kids trapped there."

"Your story seems reasonable enough when you tell it but I don't think anyone will believe you. Still, you're here and if your story is true, most of you are members of this school community. We have a large room for guests and emergencies. We can put up to 30 temporary beds in there. We are renovating the room but you can stay there for the moment. They haven't really started working on it yet. There are two working bathrooms on either side of the room. As soon as we identify if you have any living relatives we will contact them and see if they will help. Since Carly and Skylar are so close to you, I'll let them and their friends Peggy and Jade help acclimate you to this time. Tiffany can help too if her parents decide to keep her at the school. If you would like, you can attend some of our classes as guests. You can eat here as well.

"As to questions about your origins, I have a friend who runs an exclusive private school in Montana called Everest. You can all be visiting students and Rachel can be the adult sent with you. If Everest receives a call, my friend can cover our story. Everything I'm saying is temporary and subject to approval by the School Board, which as I said before I'm convening as soon as I can. Oh and we have a lost and found full of clothes. I suggest each of you select some outfits, which are from this time. And please take a bath or a shower. Some of you smell really bad. Carly, Skylar, Jade and Peggy can help you. Skylar and Carly really need a bath too." Tabatha said.

"What about me? Do you want me to live with all these girls and women, not that I really mind?" Terrance said.

"Oh yes you're the boy who tried to tamper with one of the locks and ended up in the World In Between at least that's the story. I'll call the headmaster of Briar Manor and request that he put you up at the school. I can claim you're a boy from one of the Tanglewood families that has amnesia: you can't remember anything. I'll claim your parents are out of the country and that you need a place to stay until they come back." Tabatha said.

"That's fine with me. I was after all a Briar Manor student when the witch took me into her world. Maybe the other boys will accept me if I pretend not to remember anything." Terrance replied.

"Okay I have to get going. Carly, Skylar, Peggy and Jade, I'll let you help these people get situated. I'll tell your teachers that you are on a special assignment for me and to give you a little latitude on your assignments, tests and papers. I'll also ask the teachers to allow the children here to take classes. With all the history that has passed and the changes in the world, the school material may not be easy in some respects for you but I'm guessing your reading and writing skills may actually be superior to our modern students. Anyway I realize these temporary measures may not work in the long run, particularly if the true story leaks out to the media. I'll fully brief our public affairs and parent out reach office so they can be ready to ask any questions that come our way. I just hope this plan works. I don't want to turn Tanglewood into a circus. I am hoping this is all a bad dream but somehow I don't think it is." Tabatha said as she abruptly left the table and hurried toward her office.

"Okay, Carly, Jade, Peggy and I call ourselves the Fab Four, sometimes the five when Constance is around. If we refer to each other this way you'll know what we are saying. Carly, you and I will take the girls that smell to the dormitory so they can take showers. After they are set, we will also take a shower. If I don't take one soon, I'm going to be sick. We will also bring up some clothes from the lost and found for the girls coming out of the shower to put on. Jade and Peggy why don't you try to figure out what classes everyone should be taking. Jade you can concentrate on history and literature. Peggy you can help the girls with science and math classes. You may need some remedial work in these subjects. We'll adjust your schedules depending on the abilities you show. I think you'll ace the early American History material as you lived it." Skylar said.

"Don't worry about the math. All of us studied Isaac Newton's Principia at Tanglewood and as luck would have it, this book was among the twenty we had available to us in the World In Between. Somehow the spell cast by Elizabeth caused many of Prudence's books to be drawn into the World in Between with us. Your relative Samantha certainly studied Newton. She is a math genius. Samantha makes up her own equations. Still, the rest of us have memorized Principia and indeed all the other nineteen books, which include scientific works as well as literature in Latin, Greek, Spanish, German, French, Italian and of course English. Without these books I doubt we would have survived. Because of the books we all became fluent writers and readers of these languages and very proficient in Newton's calculus. We spent countless days working on calculus equations and discussing the contents of the other nineteen books. It's amazing how much you can learn from twenty books in almost two hundred and fifty years." Beatrice said.

"Okay then we will put you in the most advanced courses in all these areas, but science may be one area where you have much to learn. Most of the science we know has been developed in the past two hundred and fifty years." Carly said.

"Okay that is agreeable to us. But I want to say one more thing before we become busy with all our new tasks. No matter what happens in the future, we will never know how to thank you enough Carly and Skylar for rescuing us from Elizabeth's prison. You've saved us from a fate worse than death. You're our heroes." Rachel said.

"Peggy and Jade helped too as did our boyfriends Cory and Thad, but your welcome. Carly and I are your new sisters. You can count on us." Skylar said.

"I know that to be true." Samantha said as she hugged Skylar with tears in her eyes.

Reflections

That evening, an over tired Skylar turned to Carly and said.

"I'm so excited about what's happened I can't sleep. Are the Key Girls really sleeping in the school's guest area? It's so hard to believe. If you told me this would happen at the beginning of the year, I'd called you crazy. On top of all that, we all have boyfriends and good ones at that who respect us. What a great year we've had. After this school year, every other year I live will be boring by comparison."

"I don't know about that. We're the Fab Four or more if you count our ghosts. I think a lot more exciting adventures lie before us. But we have more immediate problems. I'm worried that the Key Girls and Boy with the exception of Tiffany will grow old and die now that they are in the real world. There has to be some kind of natural balance. They are over 250 years old. They will eventually show that." Carly answered.

"I agree but if this happens we will have to make them as comfortable as possible and do everything we can to help them live the life they have left well. We've already promised to do that. It may be the most important thing we ever do in our life." Skylar answered.

"That's a pretty heavy thing to say. We're only fourteen after all. Still, no matter what we do from now on, I agree with you my old friend it's going to be hard to top what we just did." Carly said.

"Yeah that's true."

Skylar said pausing for a moment. Then Skylar continued.

"Is the whole thing with the Magic Keys really finished? Elizabeth is dead and her spirit has gone to an evil world. The World in Between has disappeared and only a rock wall remains where it once was."

"No, I don't think this story can be over until the Key girls and Boy die, hopefully as many years from now as us. And there is one more thing I haven't told you. Constance, Barbara and Calico told me that they still feel tremendous power coming from the area the World in Between used to be. They just arrived. Maybe they can tell you about it."

"Welcome my ghost friends. Tell me how that is possible? There isn't anything there anymore." Skylar said looking into an empty space near Carly.

"Constance has a theory. She says the World in Between existed so long as a magical place that the area it used to be has been changed. It will continue to put forth spiritual energy and attract all the magical power anywhere near it. She worries that this magic power will attract devil worshippers, witches and warlocks, who will use it as a place to conduct their ceremonies." Carly said.

"Ooh that's a little creepy but kind of exciting. I didn't know people still conducted such ceremonies. Do you think Elizabeth could ever come back from the place she is?" Skylar asked.

"I'll speak as Constance again. Once you cross over to the other worlds, you're not supposed to be able to come back but Elizabeth's master the devil, plays by his own rules. Barbara, Calico and I fear Elizabeth will find some way of returning." Carly said.

"Then the Magic Keys of Tanglewood story isn't over." Skylar said.

"Now I'm Barbara answering. No far from it." Carly replied.

"Then the super seven will deal with any problems created by the Magic Keys just as they have already done. As a team nobody can top us." Skylar proclaimed.

"I'm Calico now. You included me in the group?" Carly as Calico said.

"Of course, you faced down a ferocious bear and gave your life to protect us. That makes you a member of our group forever." Skylar said with a big smile.

"If I could purr right now I would." Calico said through Carly.

Epilogue

Elizabeth floated in the angry red and black world around her. Many souls burned in the liquid fire below. They constantly howled in pain. Elizabeth floated because she had some status here with the great one. He liked Elizabeth's dedication to confining all those kids and then ruining their lives. Elizabeth asked the great one to let her once again emerge as a spirit in the real world so she could recreate the World In Between and imprison the kids who escaped. The great one promised he would arrange it at the right time, but said that these opportunities did not come along very often. Someone from outside like his Satan worshippers would have to summon her. No being having crossed over to one of the new worlds could come back to the real world unless called. So she would have to wait along with his other favorites wanting to haunt the real world until this happened. Elizabeth accepted her master's promises. She would patiently wait for her chance to rule the World In Between again. Then she would have her revenge against the people who ruined her life including the modern girls Skylar and Carly, who are so much like the girls she hated for so long. They could never fully pay for taking her husband and children from her.